CW01511659

Mdeilmm

THE FRENCH LIST

Hélène Cixous

Mdeilmm

MOLE SPEECH

TRANSLATED BY PEGGY KAMUF

LONDON NEW YORK CALCUTTA

Seagull Books, 2025

Originally published in French as *Mdeilmm*
© Éditions Gallimard, Paris, 2022
English translation © Peggy Kamuf, 2025

ISBN 978 1 8030 9 489 2

British Library Cataloguing-in-Publication Data
A catalogue record for this book is available from the British Library

Typeset by Seagull Books, Calcutta, India
Printed and bound in USA by Integrated Books International

to Gisèle, my companion in magic
in the stairways of childhood

CONTENTS

I

THE LAST BREATHS OF THE CONDEMNED MAN

The Sentence

I was alone with Eve my mother, on the fourth floor. We were awaiting the audience for the meeting. I recited the Sentence to myself. I would pronounce it in a clear voice, without intonation, in one breath:

'Maman' —I would say, for it was to her my mother that I had to address it —

'Maman, I committed a murder'

A single line, melodic, nine syllables, each equal to the other, said in a straight and clear voice, *Maman* and *murder* having the same vocal status, *committed* having the function of a flail, no doubt would arise, I was preparing to say that

She wore shiny red shoes with high heels, stylish. They didn't fit the occasion, she didn't know it. 'Put on your flat shoes,' I say. —'Later, I will put on my sneakers,' she says. I do not say the sentence, I was waiting.

I must have called acquaintances in the middle of the night, it had escaped me: I received phone calls, people in the darkness were worrying. I didn't answer. It was Spain, it was the United

States, it was Germany. I say nothing. Embarrassed. Had I betrayed myself in the uncontrollable depths of the dream? Old habits of meetings presented themselves. I was waiting for everyone to be there in order to say the Sentence. One has to imagine it. I stand up, I turn to Eve, publicly, and I say—the way one swears an oath—

—Maman, I committed a murder—

For some reason the word *committed* was necessary. *Murder* could not be replaced by *assassination*.

It will be a blow. Everything will have instantly changed. And it will be a general test. Who will remain with me after this admission? We will see.

—No sooner does he arrive at the home of the Epantchines than the Prince puts himself in the place of a condemned man. It is the first time one hears him speak, says my son, he is in the antechamber, and it overpowers him, he is invaded by the last day of a condemned man. This day is going to last a very, very long time, says my son, like all the Last Days of a Condemned Man.

—One is always condemned to death in the great narratives of Dostoevsky I say, by penal servitude or execution, in the Karamazov trial, or in Raskolnikov's imprisonment, or in *The Possessed*, at the beginning or at the end it is always the last day, and *the Certainty*, the Guillotine is the Dispenser of these cruel hallucinations, I say

—But, says my son, the whole text of *The Idiot* is a commentary on the Last Days of the Last day

4

I don't tell my son that I had no memory of the Prince's entrance on stage, or of his first scene, or of the Epantchine house, instead there was a filtered light, and voices groping among fully living beings scattered with assassinated creatures, and even the name Epantchine had become strange to me, what remained in the memorial was the signifier Rogozhin incarnated in the howling of someone burned alive and the melodious body of Nastasya Filipovna, her ironic singer's smile,

but I hurried to consult the edition of *The Idiot* perpetually on call on my personal bookshelf, and here I am, page 25, in the little antechamber giving onto the reception room of the Narrative, welcomed by a truly novelistic sentence: 'It was already around eleven o'clock when the Prince rang at the general's apartment.' Or more precisely 11.15,

then I follow from second to second the Time of *Certainty*, an *in Pace* where the measure of blood is counted out as on the dial of a clock

Then there spreads throughout my body the sensation of being captive to a fantastic fascination. The mystery: one can't stop skimming through the pages, one after the other, one is spellbound. One hears a heavy step in the staircase, it's the Past that is coming up with a slow regularity, who is coming up, who? Who is going to enter? One continues to traverse one page after the other, because one is bewitched, one plunges into a foreign country, this very one, unknown and yet recognized and exerting hypnotic powers, one is astonished and one surrenders, one has passed a frontier without warning, it's as if one were in the Castle of a book, delivered over involuntarily, voluntarily

—Are you indeed coming from abroad? asks the servant. Whereas he wanted to ask: —Are you indeed the Prince?

—Yes, I too wonder about it, I say. On one side, I descend from a wagon. On the other, I descend from a family in extinction. I am the last of the living.

And thirty pages further on, my characters are still turning around the strangeness of this sensation of familiarity among humans, which one didn't expect and which turns out to be caused by the shared Ultimate Experience of the condemnation to death. How many differences there are between Switzerland and Russia, between the foreign land and a foreigner, differences of climate, heating, food, language, classes, customs, kinds, and among this mass of differences, as to the horror of the Last Day commanded by the *Certainty*, there is no difference between prince and servant, between you and me, between him and me, it takes merely a slight trembling of the imagination for the *Certainty* of the death of life to make one feel the indescribable freshness of its last half minute, a half minute as large as the creation-and-destruction of the world. The second the servant prince comes alive while pronouncing the Name of the Terrible Thing, a slight colouring counteracts the paleness of his face— that of the Frightened One—it is this *Certainty* that makes of human nature a single human person, the extraordinary sensation that the death of time has entered the room, there is now but a single soul alone with fading, faded hope. It is ————

It was the Past that entered. There remained of it, at this moment of the Narrative, only the heavy Step, in the stairway. I thought: so this is the Thing called Death, the step, the phantom that is left of all those beautiful, majestic forms veiled in a white mist that pass like actresses in front of the door to the waiting room, and each time one says to oneself: Is it my turn?

—And how does this frightening chapter end? I say to my son

—At the moment that a person condemned to death is knocked down by the most dreadful violence, that is, the moment his head is placed beneath the blade of the *Certainty*, the instant that says the hour, the minute the second of the severing is already in the staircase, it has twenty-one stairs to climb, already it is there, it is coming up, it is on the first landing, it knocks, walks, walks, with a cruel regularity, it still has fifteen stairs to climb, the torture lasts eternally times fifteen blows of stairs, there is still there is no more than, there is no more than fifteen thirteen characters including intervals, how deep are these chasms with their gleaming cliffs on the crest of which the soul hangs only by an elbow, one hears an exquisite ultra-sensible ultrasonic pain, one has just felt one's hair turn white and hard from terror, what happens to the body is an unknown horror, each second sets fire to a thought, the soul is a rowboat on an ocean of unleashed waves; it is not one but a hundred different vertigos that rise and fall successively at different speeds, in a few minutes or by other measures of duration one is thrashed overturned broken drowned killed for a long time multiplied in a frenzy of decapitations, what is awful is to die— that is, to not stop dying—from many sides and brains at once— as only certain madmen could attest, or Edgar Allan Poe if he had survived his fall into the maelstrom of Lofoten at 68 degrees latitude—the head suffers on its side and causes the knees and feet to suffer, especially the heart that beats twice as fast against the bars of the chest, seeking to escape from the merciless cage and in vain,

—whoever said that human nature was capable of undergoing this ordeal without falling into madness? says Prince Myshkin in a voice choked with tears.

—You? says my son, whose voice trembles a little from excitement, and I see from the open note that he remembers having one day been mad and afterwards having regretted losing the madness.

You'll find an answer on page 47 of *The Idiot*, says my son

I hurried to consult *The Idiot*. Already the idea of finding an echo of my anxiety acts like some beneficent magic, my legs almost stop trembling. I expect everything from the Superior World, as usual, books know everything, I open, page 47, and that's not it, there is a small landowner by the name Barashkov to whom fate has been particularly cruel, he is weighed down by debt, encumbered with mortgages, his manor burns down, his wife dies in the flames, we have already seen this in the Bible, that's not it, my mad witness, my rescue

—page 47 defies me with such indifference, someone has been misled, has misled me, the page has a head like a cage, I am suffocating, I skim the way one stumbles around, hopelessly, I fall on page 27, like a distress signal a sentence cries out 'Go, you are pardoned!' How a resurrection can strike you! A moment earlier I was sinking. From one page to the next, dying dies.

—Hey look, under this little stairwell, there's a door. If you push it open, you will find on the right a little recess where you can smoke, if you open the fanlight then your smoke doesn't bother anyone . . . says a character.

Oh! the taste of pardon! Our powerful life hangs on so little! A puff of smoke. The Prince and I push open the door

How one wakes up astonished, end. How astonished one is to be awake. I was as if magically cured of the hallucination that had taken me hostage, terror flees like a ghost called back to nothingness by the distant signal of the cock

There was Interruption. Salutary disjunction of times and worlds. In place of Scene 47, Scene 27. I was a prisoner: the Idea of Death had taken me hostage. She exists. Who? Death. The Idea. In truth, she will have always been there, behind the door.

Sometimes, rarely, a kind of short circuit happens: you find yourself simultaneously in two countries, the country of existence and the one of the beyond, this double experience is the worst kind of suffering for the subject, the I-don't-know-where-to-turn, what sense to make of it

there is no door. There isno. There is some Suddenly

Pardon is a lightning bolt. It falls like a sentence without verb, without article, like the spitting of gunfire. It doesn't give a damn about time and its durations. There is none.

—Go through that door and you can smoke, says the custodian of reality, page 27

—'But the Prince didn't have time to go and smoke.'

He was going to go, says page 27

Suddenly.

One was going to be able. Enter: a Suddenly

Suddenly:

—What was is not

—It was a poor dream. A poor hospital. In a poor country. I vaguely knew the doctor. A vague doctor. There was a case: a mother had a little immature boy. The child presented in the form of a large biscuit, round, thick, shapeless and inert. It was tragic. I didn't take my eyes off them. The mother, in her forties, came to get him. Such a child, arrested for many years. The mother gathered him up, wrapped him tightly in a shawl, attached him to her back. I wondered if the thing didn't suffer, but the boy made not a sound. The mother emitted numerous complaints about her fate. I felt pity. The unfinished child, the poorly baked boy I know all about that, this book that doesn't get out of quarantine.

Suddenly. Suddenly the biscuit seemed to move. The crust convulsed. Two eyes and a mouth were outlined. The mouth opened wide and formed a great cry of sorrow, mute. It was terrible. What misfortune! I remembered that this story was mine. Had I not had a son, a long time ago, and the word mongoloid like a biscuit. Do you know what this pain is? I cried out until I woke out of the dream. The mother was moving away with the biscuit boy.

I still see that poor tragic mask convulsed around the superhuman howl, so powerful that only the heart can invent an ear capable of receiving it without flinching

—I thought, says the book, that it could be me, the idiot child, the not-quite boy, the child in despair of managing to pass over into death.

At the moment I am speaking to you, between two crises, I don't think, despite all my hopes, that I can victoriously interiorize the beauty of life that is rising right before me, at my window, painted in the song of robins and cuckoos on a background made entirely of transparent light, like a visible and safe air, so mysteriously breathing that one could believe, despite our lower world shot through with plagues and pollutions, that there exists a living world above that is spared, innocent like a newborn's smile, that doesn't know death,

I think, in front of so much beauty so close to my fingers, to my eyes and of which I am deprived, merely deprived

and I say to myself that I am, like those sick poets, those poets inspired by illness, occupied to the point of obsession by the Idea of My Deaths, I am struck to my soul, I am like my Uncle Freud pursued by a little dread that surprises him at any moment anywhere and makes him ridiculous, it is a mania, a chronic visitation,

I am like the mouse who, wanting to escape from the cat that I am, rushes at a run at a surprising speed and seems to throw itself into the abyss it flees—just as the cat that I am seems to have but one mad idea, to go seek the dog it fears

The child-cry is me, the Book seized by crises of terror. Impossible to enter a chapter, at the home of friends or enemies, impossible to find again the beloved, impossible to climb a stairway, impossible to dream calmly and reach the day of ecstasy, impossible to walk in a park with a nascent feeling of paradise without the same Murderous Scene beginning again to present itself. Myself, I am surprised and frightened by it. Barely do I open my mouth, page 25, for the first time, and irrepressibly, while I am preparing to 'make the acquaintance' of the other characters, 'make their acquaintance and nothing more', as the Idiot says, there comes out of my mouth as if from some obscure region a long speech on the death penalty and I address it, without hesitating, to the first comer. —It might be to the reader, to you, to my mother, —what does it matter, I *must* report in detail the execution of the condemned man, it is inevitable, I must execute myself, this necessity in me that adheres to my heart, to my lungs, I do not interrogate it, it is partly my reason, partly the sentence of my destiny. With horror and delectation I retrace as if for the first time the distance since the last instant up to the first, so as to come back to the last, from there to the first, with my tongue and my words I suck and chew each beating and lukewarm instant like a mouse wriggling between my teeth, there is some, oh! there is some, it is a meticulous devouration, and everything happens as if my brain were the intelligent mouth of this butchery. I take delight in distinct forms of suffering.

Pick up *The Idiot*, enter. Who would have believed that this world so populated, so multicoloured, this opera had, as hidden motor, the hunger for death by execution, the insatiable—says the B—

In this narrative, so long, so anguished, so trembling and frothing, one sees that the narrator must start over several times before managing to finish the execution. Everything happens exactly like those examples of botched executions, reported by those who fight against the death penalty: those terrifying failed acts, that infernal struggle of the executioner with the head that still howls,

—how much longer to kill? How many dyings interrupted and begun again, how many suffocated pages that agonize, how many throat-slittings that end badly,

—this *Idiot* is an epileptic who cannot hope for the torture to end, there is no final crisis, one vainly waits for death, it doesn't come, it grants merely the pitiless help of madness, to death lost

—Do you how many times the Idiot leads us to the guillotine? I say to my son.

—From the first contact, says my son

It has been a month since I witnessed this scene, and I have it constantly before my eyes. I have dreamed of it at least five times, says the Idiot. Me too, constantly. That day, he tells us how one should paint a portrait of the scene. You paint just the face: you look the head in the face. One sees the whole scene on the face. It is there that the soul remains. All the rest is clothing.

Not going to betray it! Such a solitude invades it. The head is mad. Mad with rage. You cannot leave its eyes with your eyes. They convulse. They grab your gaze like drowning men, open terror-stricken mouths seek, roll, stare at you, it wants, to say something, to say a word, say, say,

—above all, don't let go of the fingers of the soul,

—read, read, begs the head

—I'm listening —I'm trying —what do you want to say?

And with all my invisible forces, I try to decipher what it confides of this agony. Finally I hear, I think I hear —'I waited so long, it had to come, it's like dying of not dying, I am angry' —says the head—angry, I turn my back to it, finally it finishes prattling endlessly while endlessly I try to finish, it comes, it doesn't come, it passes, sees my back, my eyes are sobbing, it thinks that I am sleeping, that I am biting, doesn't enter, doesn't lean down, doesn't kiss my tortured face. I let out a howl, what comes out of the sticky vomit from the throat of my soul is: Maman! But in what a state! My voice! says the terrified head, my voice is rusty! I didn't know what a hoarse wounded broken sound gushes out of an abandoned head. 'Maman' howls the howling

That is all that remains—no one—a word, rusty, soiled, which was living when I was not yet condemned. Poor head! One must find a superhuman pity not to let it drop

—And since then I see this Face again, says my son. The Face on which *The Idiot* pours all its tears. It is a book that weeps,

—It's a death that doesn't arrive at its ends. What impotence in this Certainty, I thought, ten or twenty times I hear its step in the stairway, so naturally, the whole body is an ear that strains, I expect the Invisible, page 74, page 75, and nothing, it remains to come, I am afraid of the stairway, it watches me hidden in each step, and each step is extraordinarily clear, during the fifteen or twenty minutes that elapse during the two minutes of haunted descent, I see myself undergo a great number of deaths, they are rather similar—at the beginning, one falls, one cries out, the cry is different, it frightens, one does not see the last moment. One remembers, one has this lightning time in which a thousand thoughts unfurl to form a single question: And after, what? *After*! After will he-she have a face? Where? Or?

—Do you know how many times the Idiot tries to aid death?

—Page 76, the Prince recounts the capital execution for the second time, one can't keep oneself from wanting to see again what took place only once, it is stronger than me, says the book, I start again, the condemned man is brought back (to me) just a minute before his death, in a minute I have to represent everything that has happened before this moment, everything, everything, he was in prison, etc., no point is saying his name, Legros is beyond names, his head is elsewhere and it *knows* everything, he still has a body to have the impression that an infinite amount of time remains to him to feel, the body wants to know nothing, it's the head that begins to look for its words, it wants the keys to the unknown country,

within the condemned man, it's everyone-for-themselves, all the thoughts and questions take refuge up there, in the head

—I scrutinized his face and I understood everything, but I don't have the strength to continue here, says the book. Ah! how I wish that someone else would reproduce this scene. You?

—But one must be able to paint it from within, or at least to feel close enough to the last days if not to the last hour. I don't know if I am close enough to the last hour, I thought. It depends on the days, the nights, the events and tempests of the world. Most of the beings who compose me are already on the other side, we telephone one another almost every day, that reassures me, between us, no disconnect, on this side, the side is a little bit on the other side, on another side, a certain number of powerful Breathers keep the world firmly around me, beginning with the cats. According to my dreams, I am much closer than I know how to believe.

The Assassination of Rabin

I didn't see the assassination of Rabin, I was in Paris, it was 5 November 1995, my beloved was on the fourth floor, he was writing a poem. The title would be *Limbo*. Among the ghosts and what frightens the ghosts, we are led towards a fear, a future fate, it is the Positive Negation. That is the theme that my dear prophet was borrowing from Samuel Taylor Coleridge. At these words a sentence arrives: 'I.R. is dead. I.R. has been killed'. One would need more than a chapter to describe the ways in which such an assassination happens to us. Is it a murder? It's an explosion. On 5 November 1995, it happens to us for the first time. We see nothing. We watch the funeral until three in the morning. The prayers, the speeches, the shudders of the Earth, we don't know what tears to shed. His name is Isaac. His name was. His name is.

One doesn't know which tense to choose, to lose, to save,

When will we be granted to rinse our heart with our tears?

My father is not named Isaac. His name is Jonas. I call the one-who-writes Isaac

—One would have to be as nearsighted as Kepler, as nearsighted as moles, those mute monks of Nature, to *see* the assassination of Rabin, to *see* the face of the Moon, like an old blind person contemplates the star, turning towards-her-towards-him their blind face that is all eye, one has to see the murder of the moon with the ear, contemplate-be contemplated by the Murder, I say to my son

When I had *seen* the *scene* of the assassination, says the book, I couldn't *see* the assassination, hardly had I gone to see than I saw that I was seeing the scene-of-the-assassination, I was transported to the point of ecstasy, I no longer knew where I was me, where I was him, the condemned one, the innocent, the assassination, the infernal rumbling of fate, the nervous tremblings of time, the mad eruption of the *need* to see, of the desire, the ferocious awakening of a cruel compassion,

And you, I say to my son, you saw the film by Amos Gitai, you saw this tragedy, you saw, say, you *saw*?

—It's hard, says my son

—It's not a film, I say, it's an assassination, it's not a murder

—It's hard, says my son

I see my son, hidden motionless behind the word Hard as if behind a dead wall. Hard, he says. A mute, fierce word.

—It lasts five minutes out of fifty minutes, I say.

I didn't know the calculation of the film. There is the Certainty, the end is everywhere, each minute of each minute is erected like a wall, like the frightening silence given off by clamouring, cries, wailing sirens, the ghost of the end infests every drop of every minute

Since I knew what was going to happen, I saw *the scene* at every second, you have already seen a ghost mutilated, bloody

—I can't talk about it, says my son

—The instant, very long, and even extremely long, must have lasted around a minute, but one of those minutes pregnant with the years that follow and the blind immensity of the present. The world trembled down to its vertebrae, a fever burned through the crowds

—Impossible

Impossible to be present to the present, especially impossible not to miss the instant of death. Time was going too quickly too slowly. I knew how this would end, a miserable knowledge, in vain I wanted to hang on to my son the scientist, in such circumstances there is no help, there is no son, everything is changed into wall

I felt an anguish of terrible death, at least anguish groans, moves, agitates, thrashes the heart, tears were falling on my cheeks they were hurrying, as if to escape the internal danger, death had begun. It was addressing someone, it called him by his name, 'You!'—him out of a hundred thousand candidates,

'You, there!' yes, You, the first one on the left

—Do you know what 'an anticipatory emotion' is? I say to my son. Rabin, he was dead and he was going to die. What is that called, those who are called upon to go-die, as Montaigne says.

—The called ones, says my son. We all function in the same way, as vertebrates, my vertebrae are conscious of the death of others, the Other-there, barely do I see its shadow, the rustling of the air as it approaches, than my vertebrae knock against each other, elephants weep in unison for the death of one of their own, they lament together like Roland and Olivier, each elephant catches death from the other, they die one another, no elephant can die for the other, the elephants weep to die so often,

—I worry about you, I say to my son. And I put myself in the future, later, when I will die.

—Don't worry, Maman, I am not an elephant, says my son. For me, for the logician that I am, you are already dead

—Let's return to 4 November 1995, I say. It is 9.15 at night. While I watch 'The Assassination' I watch the final act on Sunday, 11 July 2021 at 8.15 in the evening. Rabin's last hour is the first sequence in *Rabin, the Last Day* I have the oppressive sensation of walking on my head. He doesn't know he is being led to the last scene of his Story. As for me, I know it. What is the use? To know what the hero does not know, this Caesar is the only one who doesn't know and that all of Rome knows in Tel Aviv, and yet to be powerless as in one of my muzzled dreams, to be unable to intervene, to fight a duel with Destiny like Artemidorus armed with a bit of paper in Act II, Scene 3, and in vain,

We know, we suffer from knowing, we let loose the howlings of an ant

A red spider like a half-millimetre drop of blood runs across my desk as swift as a mite-sized cat, bright vivid red, it sees danger coming, it wants to let loose a red-blood howl, 'don't go there! Watch out for Brutus! keep your eye on Cassius! if you are not immortal, you will live!' You will recognize a spider ant by its vivid red glow, hundreds of thousands of mites hurl grey cries, we see destiny swarming from the gangway of the gods, Artemidorus has slipped up there with his anguished camera, it looks like an alarmed donkey, the camera would like to kick, 'we are flies for the gods,' says Shakespeare, 'and I have nothing to do with it'

—I am dreadfully sad, I say to my son, it is 9.25, unlike the spider that rushes like a quick red missile, I am paralysed, 'that he shall die, we know,' it is necessary to die to the end. Can you explain the brain of a spider, who knows and doesn't believe what it knows?

Rabin speaks. He is lively. He resembles the Idiot in the First Part of the novel. He speaks, thinking he is addressing human beings, he addresses, the crowd,

I'm afraid, he is enjoying the crowd-soul, he is mad, I say to myself, he believes, I say to myself,

—beware of phenomena of emergence, whines the vivid red spider

—take a hundred thousand individuals, squeeze them into purée in a saucepan, individual behaviour disappears, the crowd-soul boils with huge bubbles

Rabin's last words

escape me

The last words escape me to the point of nostalgia

the last message, the key, the germ and the promise

as if he were not there at the last word and there is no one to say it

Instead—but that's not it—there were three sharp shots with no echo—like three raps on the door of nothing. One had time to hear them because there were three. At the first shot, one wonders—the second confirms, the third countersigns the process. —Heard heard? Yes—Yes, yes, that's indeed it, the assurance of the impossible.

I was following Death. Death is coming. It takes its time. One doesn't see it. One hears it. It's gasping. It speaks in rattles, it advances with great rattles. Extrahuman prattles. That is what frightens us: the non-form, the ungraspable presence, the rustle of a cold wind, this force that makes its faceless way, like a secret army from all sides, this imminence that looms like a fit of epilepsy, which cannot be opposed by weapons, or ramparts or flight, a giant exhaled from a giant chest,

—how big?—vast, like the Ocean raised up comes to crush its Earth, like the enormous soul of Torture

of the enormous size of the blade of the guillotine when it rushes all of a sudden at its prey, throws itself, for it is animated, a blade tall like a wave of steel, a collapse of severing metal like an infinite razor

meanwhile designated the victim stirs vivid red frenzy,

the horror is the duration, it is perpetual, it hollows out the brain in the unknown depths of metres and metres of inflamed pain

Who could describe to whom this maelstrom of hallucinations?

—I can't, says my son.

The Voice of my son is like a fallen tree which my drunken distress would like to grab onto but the delirium is a torrent that mocks my pitiful desires

'the blade,' I can almost manage to proffer its sounds

Bablade, sputters my tongue

—a monstrous alteration of all perceptions that I am alerted to only by the cruel jolts of some of my dreams, by the rare and precious testimony of those who have survived a death sentence, but precisely those who have already been dressed in the mortuary garment, those who are already costumed as cadavers, whose head is covered with a white hood and whose limbs are chained and who at that moment are seized by veritable rage to have done with it, suddenly a devouring hunger for the end, and who would like to cry out: Quick! Quick! Quick. But there is no Quick, it is then that the pardon falls like a blade, and not the reverse—too late,

from now on one will die life, too late: one can no longer send death away, it sticks to the heart and especially to the brain, immortal illness, from now on daily, disgusting insect crouching in the hippocampus, it haunts and multiplies, it even has, it seems, its preferred moments—it likes to crawl under the skull in the morning upon waking,

—What's the matter, says my son, are you drooling?

—I'm sinking, I say. It's this subject.

I am astray, since forever, in unbreathable regions, I feel as weak as a ghost, all I do is stir up a sombre thick heavy air, a day doesn't dawn, the space is invaded by a madness of papers, rustling of my ghostly feet that walk on nothingness

I try to indescribe what has happened to me since I fell into the whirlpool of the Last Days, I am totally conscious of struggling in the Other Reality, what makes me despair is the fear of never being able to return to the good side, on an A4 sheet of paper, welcoming, clean, like a window, I wriggle about in vain

the worst thing is that I don't recognize myself, the trees that have always been my saving saints have lost their powers. My oak, my pine, pass in front of me as if I were a cadaver, the growing light does not illuminate me. I lower my head: I am within as if I were cut off separated from my body. Thus what cannot happen happens

—One has only one wish: to be shot, says the Idiot

I recognize him! It sounds just like the voice of my son. Well, believe me, it is as if all of a sudden a little air came back to me, through my ear, it's as if I heard all of a sudden the voice of my father which I lost one day in February 1948

it's as if I heard Rabin's last word

it's as if I heard the last word of Humanity

One morning in July, I heard a sound of a wardrobe, I shudder as if thrown outside of my head, like the moment of exultation when I heard a donkey bray, said the Prince, one evening in Basel, me the groan of an animated wardrobe. I was lost, I was wandering, says the Prince, my consciousness straying, when suddenly in the dark, in Switzerland, the groaning complaint of a donkey, so precise, so familiar, like the deep timbre of my father. Saved! I say to myself, life is over here!—Me, my donkey is the cat. The rapid light little step of busy Isha, like the voice before the voice, then the cooing, then the little face lit up by those two shining eyes, like a birth out of nothingness. That is what Pardon is. One cannot hope for it: it is wild. It is absurd and free, free, it is hidden in a wardrobe, in the shofar of a donkey, in the sound of the horn of an old Citroën that rings out from the main post office all the way to the gates of the city, in a word shining like the persistent look of a cat.

There were three sharp shots, and a vertiginous immortality began

It was the eleventh minute in the blackness, a long interminable minute like those infernal buildings whose exit door one cannot find, one goes down, down, the abyss swallows the minutes of the minute one after the other. One hears death swallowing when it swallows the crowd like a soup of ants, one hears it eating time, growling, chewing the sounds, reducing existences to purée, swallowing the world: it's a hearse in black and white that fills the horizon of the screen, drawn by four Impassive Fates, without stopping, without haste, with the dreadful slowness of the Ceaseless.

One can no longer hear the dialogues of life resonating, the human henhouse has fallen silent, people don't know that they are in the overstuffed stomach of the end, they are sinking in countless numbers, they are sunk, what is that, that smothered sound of shards of voices? it is what was the crowd and the crushed words, that ensilted sound that grazes the eardrums of the indifferent planets,

instead of air, a sticky fog

it is darker and darker, the ants are raging more and more and in vain, and it is then that three pointed, sharp, hurried seconds pierce like the angry cry of a blind cock

—How do you spell that? I say to my son. The Cry?

—Like this: Bang! Bang! Bang. The silence is pierced

—Just before Bang, says the Idiot, one can hear a clicking of scales: it's the ffrrssttt. No one had heard that before: the ffrrssttt of the blade that coughs. It lasts a half second, one might not have noticed anything. By contrast, cries of Horror leap out in bursts of fireworks. One witness notes: 'What a Horror.' Everyone in all languages is in agreement on this word. The witness notes this word in his notebook. Horrible horrible horrible. The third time the word bursts out like a sob. The cries rise—all words are turned to dust—fall, clash, shout the earthly circus. Suddenly people understand that they are piled in a tomb

If I had the strength of the author of *A Descent into the Maelstrom* or of Gustav Mahler, I would describe here the Last Breaths of the Last Day of Isaac Rabin. Every breath is a struggle between Life and Death, these two invisible fighters. All the mythological hand-to-hand battles that have been waged in human memory come to watch and witness these last ones. And each time, it is that passionate embrace between Love and Hate, between the Prince and Rogozhin, between the soul and Fate. One no longer sees what is in Dispute. Between Achilles and

Hector who draw our gazes lies the Thing stretched out, deformed, that still is. Not another word! It is Breaths that here replace words.

There were three shots . . . and the Thing began to be there, everywhere, the invisible, the minutes seized by panic,

Thanks to the cat, I jumped off the train of time between the eleventh and twelfth minutes. I leapt out of my study as out of a nightmare and went down at a run at the risk of falling into the gullet of the stairwell, to get a coffee, as if I were being chased by an assassin.

I come back to the donkey.

The Breaths, it's the donkey! The last word, naked, struggling, denouncing the imbecilic injustice of fate, the call, the salute. It is the Messiah. There is a battle. A Force tries to crush a Force. The soul grabs on, pleads, testifies, repeats. All around, on the Place of Kings, there is Racket and Pandemonium. We are attacked, distracted, deported. We who didn't want to let go for one second of the hero of Humanity, the best of us. Suddenly we hear that we no longer hear that sob of the Fighter, that heavy breathing. A sob didn't arrive. The ear that we are gapes open, in vain. It doesn't come. The donkey, the horn, the child, everything that cries is silent, or else it is my deafness, my weakness, my laziness? I lost the ultimate one? Or it's my human deficiency, we didn't know, didn't grasp, didn't receive, didn't save the last sign. We let it fall into the abyss?

I must absolutely go back in time, when we were at the instant before the separation, the instant when everything is at stake

Here is the instant: it strikes three sharp blows, like the two little blows of Moses' rod on the rock

Bang! Bang! Bang! That way one is sure not to miss losing the Promised Land. And—Bang!

—And already Isaac Rabin is-not-yet-dead, eight minutes of this immortality remain, and who knows it? how vast and minuscule are the eight minutes and in each measure of the beating how many minuscule and immense lives and deaths, and how many resurrections, and how many alreadys in each not-yet, in eight minutes four hundred and eighty lives die, four hundred and eighty dead ones try desperately to bite, perhaps

but he, the victim, perhaps, he is living a thousand deaths-lives, and he is alone in his fight

Meanwhile

—Is this agony going to last a long time?

—Who is complaining? I say, moved to tears. But it is the donkey who complains, with its voice like a car horn, I say to myself

According to the Idiot, this powerful braying is that of Christ. According to me, this braying crosses the city and reaches as far as my study, it's the voice of my father, the one that wanders desolate among the stars since the last hour of Thursday, 12 February 1948

—And since that date, I say, I stubbornly seek the last words, all those keys that the sages and the saints have left us at the moment of the last of the last breaths, at the instant of the cut, that instant when the outcome is still undecided and already the Traveller sees what he has never seen before

—The Revelation? says the Idiot. It happens between the guillotine and the one condemned to death. Like the word *to*, the most discreet and powerful word of all our works of thought, the magic key of Syntax, to, the word of movement at a stand-still

—If only the guillotine could speak, I say.

—When, in the place of one man like another, there is man no longer, there is the destituted one, the condemned one, the unknown one destined to hand-to-hand combat with the monster, the destinedead,

—I can't talk about it—says my son, all closed up, doors closed, gaze withdrawn

—What the condemned one perceives, I say, in the last I-don't-know-what-minute-second-of the candle

—I can't talk about it, says my son.

—Perceives? says my daughter. How do you spell that?

—I have shivers, says my son.

—It's a gigantic tarantula, says the Dying Hippolyte, it can be compared to a scorpion that will never have existed in nature, an envoy from the other world, a deaf dark and mute being, a reptile, a ghost come to my home *Expressly*, formed of serpents, brown in colour, running at extraordinary speed despite its carapace, brown, but it is not a scorpion, it's obvious that the monster is a unique species *Expressly* that hides in the wardrobe *Expressly*, it's its rustling that rattles in the wardrobe, its tails that twirl at top speed

—mine, I say, appears in the guise of a man of average height, as to speed it is extraordinarily slow, it climbs the walls very slowly, it rattles in the stairwell, I'm afraid that it will slip under the pillow, what tortures me the most is its silence, I cannot help but feel a mystic terror of this silence, when I think about it, it has two red arms, its head is a tongue as sharp as a razor, its chest is empty, without lungs, without heart, without ribs,

—that is exactly it, a non-creature, animal, all-powerful, says my daughter

—so this is how it materializes, this stranger that I have continued to watch since it entered the chamber of our life as a repugnant roommate? I murmured. And I was careful not to specify the identity of this reptile, the only way not to admit it into my head

—That is exactly She, says my daughter, or else He without any doubt, it is

—I can't talk about it, says my son

—to each their scorpion, I say hastily, mine has always been mute and venomous, and distant. In all circumstances, the Thing has stayed several steps away from me as if the secret of its power were in its distance. When my father was taken away in front of my eyes the execution was done without a sound without a word, as if everything were happening behind a thick glass

—Without a word? says my daughter.

—He was perhaps already dead, I say, and we didn't know it. What was my father was attached to me by the eyes

—But before the silence?

—When the blade falls, says the Idiot, it is not the last moment. When the severed head grimaces, it wants to speak, it speaks, it says, and no one hears, there is no vocalization, there is no air, no one. No one will ever be able to say what it's like.

—I saw my father's mouth move, my eyes cried out: what are you saying?, despairing,

—That is totally nightmarish, says my son

—He is still speaking. And I don't hear it! I'm listening and I don't hear

—Cerebral death is not instantaneous, says my son

—He is not dead! I cried. I was furious

Death is not death, I say, it still goes on. When the blade [*lame*] throws itself into its journey

—How do you spell *lame*? says my daughter

—It's a moment of absolute confusion, everything happens between blade and soul, *lame* and *l'âme*, in gigantic proportions,

—I can't talk about it, says my son. Seriously I don't want to think about that. Thought is overtaken by pure terror.

At the last moment

My father-and-I were

a single being cut in two

A violent fit of abandonment took hold of us, each one on their own side, the head, the body, we cried mutely: —you're abandoning me! you're abandoning me! —How can you abandon me? —a curtain of opaque fog rose from the depths between us, separated us, I resented my father, some reproach was rising from my feet up to my belly in nausea, for its part my head cast looks of a bitterness that made me despair

such is the pain unleashed under the blow of separation, a pain of unhappy sadness

—It makes me tremble with horror, says my son

—A terrible reproach on both sides. My father's look of anger, against which all of my reproaches rebelled, eternally. This scene never stops repeating

It was the last minute before the Breaths, we didn't know it, we saw a word cast a pale and gentle light on Rabin's face, it must have been one of those words of gratitude to humanity that spread that delicate tinge on a beloved face, as when I declare 'I love you' to my daughter and in return she thanks me whereas it is I who have just said to her 'thank you for humanity', it is this luminosity that animates the Idiot in the moments of ravishment. And right at that precise moment when the words

Thank You lit up the world, and in the hubbub, one could read it on the Face

—I suppose his sentence was cut off, says my daughter

—He had said his last word, I say.

—What was it?

—The word that no one believed. Except him. It's as if he had just said Thank You to Life

—It was Shalom!

—The moment the blade was launched, the word destined to betrayal the name of the breath, the soul

That flees

The body, sheds its clothes, beginning with the shoes, looks for, the exit

—What minute is it? she murmurs directly to the heart, her lips on the ear of the heart

Meanwhile the streets pass outside rumbling, giant wails rise through the night, it is rivalling sirens. An anguish surrounds me and throws me off-balance

—I can't get out of this page, I say to my daughter, it holds me in its guillotine arms, it's ridiculous. There is something malevolent in this frightful mute din, as soon as I approach the arena a force of attraction is set off, draws me in, binds me, if I hear the howls of the inaudible, it's because they echo within me, do you hear me? you, do you hear me?

A doubt pushes brutally against my back: is my daughter in real reality, external, free, tangible? Or in the other, in my head, simulacrum, effigy, deceptive aspect of rescue? And where has the time gone? Drop by drop, and sometimes by spoonfuls, it pours out, red of an incredibly bright red, I would never have thought that dying required so much blood

—is this blood going to last, this red chant gone astray?

—I am in the state of Gustav Mahler, I say, internally besieged by the last gestures of the Adieu, life has just left, remains the Breath

and now, where do I go?

—Where are you going?

That is always the Question, the first and last, the motionless door, the thirteenth minute, its idiotic whirling

—Where are we going? says the Idiot

the anguish of the last second before the last second, the fear of being born otherwise, the leap and the abandonment, the long blood, the sob of life in life, the cold that methodically bites the body, the heart that watches motionless and awaits its second

—in Mahler's state, —I say to my daughter, when he tries to cope with the torrent of loud racket, he does not want to die before having exhaled his last loving word

—The word, was it indeed heard?

One could read this phrase on Yitzhak Rabin's face. His face had always been calm, calmly handsome, its traits well defined, his eyes attentive with something gentle and surprised in their gaze, a trembling of welcome mixed with alarm, rather pale, and it's especially the mouth that was surprising, the childlike smile that escaped from the lips and as if from the prudent surveillance of the gaze. He always ended up by saying yes.

—How do I do it? I say. I write: dead?

—Cut! says my daughter.

—I have cut.

It was twenty-six years ago that Rabin's Breath was lost in the night riddled with blows of flares and the howls of cameras. Nobody heard him, he disappeared in the din of the world.

—What relation are you drawing between the man condemned to death and Rabin? says my son.

—It's a matter of Isaac's paradox, I say. He is blind and he sees his own death every day. What distresses him is not to see what is looking at him, and to see that he does not see what he thinks he sees

—Which Isaac are you talking about?

—Isaac, the one who calls me back endlessly, I lift the receiver—I don't even need to lift the receiver, I have his voice recorded in my soul—and I hear him repeat the agreed-on message: 'Remember, we owe Asclepius a cock'

—And you remember?

—And every day I am recalled, and I recall to myself the last days. It's a matter of the Last Day. When one Day this day arrives, I recognize it, I think, and—no question of losing the least bit of it.

I don't want to lose death, I say. I want everything, I want the last word. After the word, I want the breaths right down to the last one

—That you see him pass is not impossible, says my son.

—I localize Rabin's last breath, I say, with the greatest precision, around 11 minutes 15 seconds into the recording.

With my whole body, with my various ears, among which my eyes, my fingers, my lungs, I busy myself circumferencely with the last days that the last instants last, I am very close, all ears, knowing that it is around here that time leaves us in the lurch

I listen, I hear. I hear. I hear. I no longer hear. The Breath is drowned in an explosion of noises, cries, sirens

Lost

So I return to writing around this missing instant, I play with the trace as Mahler's Earth begins again to begin again.

—I don't remember my dead, says the voice of Isaac to me. And he has, in this case, the voice of a boy coming from the football stadium, clear, feverish, accelerated. I don't remember, it's you, with your hunt for butterflies, who provoke reminiscence in me. One day, fifty years ago, I was. I was coming out of the football stadium, I had to take the tram, I run, I throw my bag and football shoes to have my hands free

—And —?

—Let's drop it.

—You always want to drop it when one gets to the essential thing

—Cut

I find myself, I find myself me, in a police station. I woke up with cops around me, I saw the scene. I was watched over like a newborn or a newly dead. I was not him. I must have regained consciousness. Slowly. Didn't know where I was. No subject. Didn't know who I was. Knew nothing. No consciousness. No memory. None. Neither. It is others who patched the story together: I had taken, that tram, a truck arrived. I woke up before me, without me.

The terror began the next day.

Let's change the subject. I don't remember. It's you who reawaken this non-story, with your hunt for palpitations.

—Let's change the subject, I say to my son. Obviously I have forgotten everything. It's my notebook that remembers.

II

THE DEATH-SKIMMERS:

OBITUARIES

We brush up against death. As for you, you frequented it, it was your fate. Had I known that your life would be as short as you used to say. I didn't go along with your premonition. I defied your fears. I had bought death off. I had already more than once greased its palm. Sacrificed a son, a father, a dog, a cock, especially males. Generations of aunts, cousins, friends. Enough

You thought only of her. She was of a feminine gender in French. But you never told me her name. She was there, in your language, like your shadow, your internal companion and your curse.

What if one had to choose between a brief and glorious life and a long life but without glory? How to choose between two lives?

Eve my mother doesn't hesitate: whoever wants to travel far takes care of their mount. She advises you to choose the long journey. The wise man avoids glory. If one listened to him.

—I would choose rather the long life, says my daughter.

How to explain this fate? An election, like an undiscussed, undiscussable ambition? In the series of mythological metamorphoses, to see oneself destined to the imperial crown, the immortality that follows death. Choose? that is to say, taste, seek with one's tongue the pleasure in life or in dying—and finally choosing kills it also, one cannot choose without losing a life

Peace, that is the last word that the hero addresses to all those who are present that night and all those who are not present but who are there otherwise. The absent ones of all sorts. And the dead with whom communication is not interrupted. I remember that you had repeated the word 'Shalom'. 'The man that I am would like to be a Cat and sleep,' I don't recall if you said that but I know that you thought it

PEACE.

This word awakened in me a heartrending desire to find our last word. A serious burning fear, of having committed a murder by forgetfulness, negligence, sacrilege. As if I had lost the talisman that you gave me to keep eternally. I received this word at 9.30 on the night of the 11th to the 12th, I remember each instant, I ran, I waited, I watched, I was stretched out on the back of time, it was monstrous, I was not sure, I listened to no thought, I gave myself no hope, I waited, I noted everything down, my handwriting was firm and tenacious like a sword, I was not going to let myself by conquered, I have totally forgotten our last words, but my notebook saved them. The poor things, they have slept alone for so many years. When I approached the wardrobe—a gesture that it never occurred to me to make— as if now had arrived the day of revelation, my heart beat with a timid joy. The joy that takes hold of Ulysses when, in Book XI of the *Odyssey*, he arrives at the cemetery that Tiresias guards. And there they are, those who were sleeping, who crowd among the pages.

And do you know what his last word was? I say to my daughter, —he was yelling and breathing in the telephone as in ivory horn, he was afraid that his cracked voice would not manage to cross the stream of shadows, I was awfully afraid he was going to burst a vein 'Be careful of your throat,' I say —and I said, and he said:

News and messages from the dead reach us naturally without taking account of our postal chronology. That is what makes for their force and authority: they liberate us from the tutelage of the calendar and its artificial and ephemeral order, and that is how they invite us to the benefits of eternity.

Our eternity is made up of rebeginnings. I can relive each one of its measures like the movements of a symphony, they are lives, like plays in Shakespeare's work, I can choose *The Tempest* or *Antony and Cleopatra*, like I can choose Book XI of the *Odyssey* or Book XXIV, and each time it's another pain and another joy

What suggested to me to repeat the 1992 life is the cover of the notebook that shelters it: it is buttercup yellow, brilliant, promising like a Moleskine

H reviews the first pages and the last. On Tuesday, 8 December 1992, she waits for him a long time, worried, haunted by childhood reminiscences. Traversed by the coming and going of desire. Time is lost minute by minute. You there finally. He looks at her. You look at me. Across the vast room. It's a look of congratulation. Congratulated, the body is moved. Everything is good today. The warm bedroom perfumed by Schumann. It's good? Hair (his) treated with a lotion twice a day, the man child is serious. Serious, she listens, praising. This time it's he who wants, who wants. To be her, to be caressed, overthrown by her who almost faints on him. That evening it is the other version, she grabs, she gets drunk, she gets, she panics. The beautiful wild face, the jaw cruel, the pleasure hard, or lasting, sought-after, painful, returned, makes for a good so hard, so high,

both of them sleep, his sleep, her sleep. She wakes up and prays, asks for eternity and grace, it's because he is her life. Getting dressed in the gentle exchange, then

she shows him the telegram that is still so alive, so terrible. As having just happened. Its arrival drew tears from her that morning.

One didn't expect it: it appears to be but a desk drawer. One opens it and suddenly there is resurrection. Here slept for more than a century a memorial the size of a scarab, in which hibernate stories of grandeur and illusion, a paper cenotaph 20 centimetres by 10, a tomb empty of one who died for the History and Dreams of the country of Europe. The body of the dead one is buried in a forest without address, where it returns, has returned to the Belly of the mother. Meanwhile the book of his soul is preserved in this shatteringly sober summary. All the mysteries of war and passions of humanity—all the traits of the primitive scene of Passion, and the origin of Tragedy—are engraved in this paltry, unique monument. The briefest of funeral chants. The saying of the Life and Death of the infantryman Michael Klein. The soldier is dead. Dead from war, dead from illusions and hostilities, death of an ant for the anthill, Antmichael Klein. Every soldier is in contention for death. All sign up for the Trojan War. The soul remains with the women

The remarkable feature in the text of the cenotaph is the respect for the forms of the ceremony: the sentence must be faithful to the rules of the service. It follows orders. It is endowed with fateful powers like wedding rites.

It occurs to her that the telegram is a wedding announcement for Antmichael Klein with the god emperor of Error. There is something blinding in the realm of men.

—I am on the side of widows, she thinks.

—I don't understand this adultery, says my mother. What is it they find in war? If your father had listened to me, and your sweet friend?

My sweet friend is contemplating himself in the mirror of the telegram.

—Here is a testimony, he says. He reads and rereads for a long time, attentive, serious. We are now in July 1916. It is Michael Klein who has just died. She tells him about the star of David in the Byelorussian forest and the iron cross in his hand.

He notices the genealogical twig. Deciphers with difficulty the gothic handwriting —Helene Meyer —Ah! You are a Meyer. And an Ehrenstein. In the distance, the forest of names grows more and more dense. The light is soft in 1992, as in 1916. She recounts the scene of her father's silence behind the glass of the last day.

He listens. He hears. I wonder if you love me because of these condemned fathers. Because I am the most mortal of all men. You must have felt it. No one is like me, so hunted. Not one instant without that thought. In the street, I look at every 'after' as if it were the last time. I never get into my car without thinking it is perhaps the last time. Every hour, the last. I receive the telegram, and I weep. You must have felt that

I say: no.

—We are repeating the old scene

—No, I say

—Or else you induce in me this scene, this silence (without my knowing it, without your knowing it)

—No.

—Rabin's last look, strangely tender, I say to my daughter

—Someone in me may think that I must not break this silence. Who knows, if I spoke instead of the silence, what a catastrophe, an explosion.

—No.

—One has to renounce, she says. Two dangers: renouncing

too much, renouncing not enough. Often I renounced you too much, she says. Or else sometimes not enough. In the end, I would not have renounced.

—It will always be like that, he says, perhaps. *Endlessly*. I give you that word

He says 'endlessly' in his language, according to him it's less dangerous.

My daughter reads the Yellow notebook. We are now in 2020 —It's not a journal, she says. Half the time you are in the third person.

Except for a moment where one of the two of you says *I*.

The dead accompany me. I do not live without my dead. The dead write to me. Without writing we would not have been able to exist or survive. My father would have turned pale and disappeared into the fog. I hear my mother stirring the air in the kitchen with her categorical phrases while I see her walk down the main alley to go conquer the market. She is a decisive woman shot through with worries and disapprovals, without any hesitation: according to her, one must do everything so as to live in the present, that's the ambition, there is no other time but life. She completely disagrees with many of the people she meets in my study, Socrates, cousin Pons, Kafka, Achilles and moreover all those soldiers, her father who dies for Germany, my father, if he had listened to her he would not have died by France, and don't forget to disconnect the battery of the car when you leave, that is one piece of advice that does not provoke disagreement. Disconnect reconnect. What is finished is finished says my mother, what is finished continues I say. I write so as to continue, the birds at dawn still dark at this hour would not exist if I didn't hold out the paper and the pen so as to hear their affirmations in their language. Time is above all the truth of time, its truths independent of our prejudices, which the birds take care to remind me of as any other being allied with the birds and with writing. We, people of houses and prisons who are conjugated in the imperfect.

My whole life is in the present, my memory is an immense wardrobe full of the dead and eternities of my lifetime, we are naturally anachronistic, and everything will always have been written in the present in my notebooks. I have been writing ever since I was. My notebooks are the boats that have always helped one cross the Lethe. One can never say enough the degree to which paper, this very light material, is solid. It is, like writing, some very powerful nothing. I write that is to say I get on board a notebook to cross abysses and be reborn from the fires. The notebooks are like dogs or cats: a great love unites us, a strong pact like an oath, up to the last page. What moves me each time is the last day of the notebook, the last vision, the sail that reaches the distance in the painting and is the portrait of the adieu.

One day I will write a book composed solely of the last pages of my notebooks. It will be like the last looks of Argos, the one who passes into immortality looking into the eyes of the beloved.

Sometimes it is necessary for me to begin again one of our lives, I choose one at random, having no preference, having no favourite, I go by chance. What a discreet and friendly pleasure to make our acquaintance. As I am no longer that person who is burning at my place in the notebook, how she astonishes me, I follow her with my heart as if my heart were her mother, she does as she likes, according to her extreme needs, an extremist of passion. After several experiences of this reading plunged in the fire, I who am now of a more frugal generation, I would say if someone asked me the question that I feel tenderness for the characters of these notebooks, sometimes I marvel as one may at those who fearlessly take the dizzying risks of adoration, in zones where the climate violently changes beyond morality, not immoral but divinely hypermoral where one doesn't hesitate to venture antarctically or to withdraw on occasion into the arms of a prehistoric forest—extraordinarily intense sojourns in an extratemporal dwelling that we leave still shivering, in order to return to the obligations of the post-1950s era, still shaken and nostalgic for the belly of the Earth, to which we count on returning in secret as soon as possible

If there were not the notebooks to preserve these traces of ages with their biblical humours, I would be orphaned of my thrones and my tombs

I had some fifty notebooks with Isaac. There is enough to relive up to my last day. I do not count them. I do not know them. When I need the chances of a song, I reach out my hand in the night. The notebooks are not arranged, they crowd together in disorder, I seize a moment of the endless feast and then I receive our news

Obituaries

Yesterday I received a death notice that I would never have expected. I received it 'with-stupefaction'. It's as if I had received my own death notice, or that of Ulysses. My father died, one does not get over it. That's what death is: one doesn't believe it. And it's now that this arrives! There is a little girl in me who doesn't believe it, it's her decision and I respect it, she has never given in, whereas I, without believing or not believing, I have gone along my whole life disarmed with my father expiring behind my back. And then here, so late, while it's for me now that an obituary is being prepared, the notice arrives. How much time it will have taken between 'he is dying' and 'he is dead' and then between 'he is' and the word dead, a word that is never dead, that goes on baring its teeth, that doesn't let go of its ambiguities. Myself I have never had done with dying my father. Afterwards, none of my life-beings who were carried off as victims is dead to me. One lives this sorrow otherwise

That my father died is my fate, it goes on between my heart and my brain. Until this day I had not received the public verdict on it. I had left it there, in that strange fixed dimension, our first visual creation, where my father was in majesty in the background of the picture, tall and silent like a god, only his eyes spoke to me, not his mouth, I began at that arrested instant to learn to read, everything brought us together, the uncrossable distance, the meeting of looks, the words of explanation that didn't exist and that my thought felt pass by while murmuring beyond its reach, and I, who enveloped this whole vision in the dimensions of a temple, I was within as small as must have been, I imagine, the prophets the size of an insect when they were convoked by God. No doubt because of these outsized and unusual proportions, I instantly stopped paying no attention to the eternal Presence of my father and, naturally, from one day to the next, I took him for god. And then, to my stupefaction, a sensation of early childhood, in truth, more than seventy years having passed, I receive a public and civic notification,

I thought, and I was in the state of Kepler, someone whose vision was as poor as my own—there that's for you, says my son the scientist, Kepler an infinite mortal whose numerous diplopias and myopias did not prevent from seeing what was happening in the streets and ports of the moon—all of a sudden I saw what was happening to me in several worlds at once and I saw my father in several simultaneous realities. All of a sudden his death was a Fact. It was engraved in the newspaper.

—Fact, says my daughter, what a word!

—A word my father gave me when I was five or six years old, when he was pedagogically revealing to me the Extraordinary Words. We were walking along the railings of the Military Circle in Oran and he was transmitting to me one by one the keys of the language, unlimited kingdom. With *Fact* you can do anything, even make someone die. That was at the beginning of writing. That for Montaigne it was one of the fairy words of his childhood in the nursery I learnt only much later.

At that time, the time of apprenticeship, my father was still that high young man with an exhilarating and Homeric presence and we were on the same side. He rose like the sun, an indubitable fact.

The event of this year is the arrival of the Notice, and afterwards the mystery of the life of the Notice, a mole's life. One will thus have lived more than seventy years on earth, going coming, growing and shrinking, already the children of our children are forgetting us have forgotten us far off in time, meanwhile trampling beneath our steps this life that is so hidden beneath the immortal earth, meanwhile it digs, it will have dug and dug, and it's on Wednesday 29 December 2020 that the mole surfaces as at the end of a Journey in the Belly of the Earth.

That day the messenger is my cousin. The fateful postman is that character that no Greek or Shakespearean tragedy can do without, the porter of life or death, without which I myself when I happen to act as writer for the theatre would be reduced to desperate powerlessness. This self-unaware divinity and as omnipotent as the pollinating insects to which we owe *Sodom and Gomorrah*, that improbable and providential insect that comes to visit the offered and neglected pistil, me, is my cousin. And as if she were obscurely aware of this unimaginable mission, she had spontaneously dressed and decorated herself with the hairdo of an ambassador chosen to deliver to an addressee whose blossoming is threatened by fatigue weakness, diminished vitality, an unhoped-for viaticum. Those who have had the bitter experience of extinction-resurrection, who like Kafka have died more than twenty times before death and who have awakened from that nightmare with a burst of laughter, will understand me.

What the Ambassador takes out of her basket: in the *first place*, a thermos of hot chocolate that is half-emptied, since we are in a play by Chekhov, it fell over on its belly and vomited

a dozen large sheets of paper yellowed by time, covered with lines traced in a writing of a massive size without paragraph, sometimes placed in a pharmacy agenda dated from the beginning of the last century, called 'The Communications', folded stuffed into a plastic sleeve that used to be transparent, now grimy dull old, placed in another dirty folder containing

on the one hand the document called: *Obituary*, an original on that newspaper paper whose letters have not changed in the hundred years since it was created, also yellowed, old and yet still solid, of the exact size of the gold scarab, the beautiful and mysterious Scarabaeus, having remained unknown and of an inestimable value in its insect appearance, as one will recognize here:

❋

NÉCROLOGIE. — C'est avec stupéfaction que nous avons appris le décès du docteur Georges Cixous.
Ce jeune médecin, après avoir exercé son art dans notre ville, s'était depuis deux ans installé en Alger.
Sa conscience professionnelle et son affabilité lui avaient valu l'estime générale.
Le racisme hitléro-vychiste n'est pas étranger à ce décès prématuré.
Nous présentons à Madame Georges Cixous, à Madame Samuel Cixous, à M. et Mme Amar ainsi qu'à toutes les personnes que ce deuil affecte nos condoléances profondément émues.

❋

*
**

OBITUARY. —It is with stupefaction that we learnt of the death of Doctor Georges Cixous.

This young doctor, after having practised his art in our city, had moved two years ago to Algiers.

His professional conscientiousness and his affability earned him general esteem.

Hitlero-Vichyist racism is not unrelated to this premature death.

We offer to Madame Georges Cixous, to Madame Samuel Cixous, to M. and Mme Amar as well as to all those whom this loss affects our deeply felt condolences.

*
**

At the moment I felt a delirious emotion, as if I had just seen in reality Legrand's extraordinary scarab, a fantastic metamorphosis of my father in the newspaper. It is always the same mystical behaviour close to trance that incites the appearance of this coleopterous insect, this immemorial sleeping creature that looks like a pebble the size of a walnut, it's a mouse, but not electronic, but sacred: one didn't know but guesses that this format contains the archive of a people, a country, a continent, a History, of one of those heroes of the beginnings of our humanity, a pioneer of thought, an explorer of the ultimate enigmas, in the mould of Enkidu, and in this case this envoy from life to death was my father. No one could be mistaken about it.

In general, these missionaries of the mysteries do not remain on earth very long, they are mortals like you and me, one is quickly worn out by sounding the depth of caves

I trembled, but I said nothing to my cousin the Ambassador, in quests, Ambassadors, astonished friends, the guardians of treasures, are all innocent,

it's my cousin Saul, the dwarf, the unknown descendant of a great nation of guardian dwarves, the halfwit archivist, who cut out the little Newspaper scarab and preserved it, for a perpetual duration, in the dusty amber of his old boxes, among the notices of births, deaths and diverse genealogical events. So he had carefully cut out the death's head sphinx, trimmed, cut down, reduced to the absolute event thus sublimated: took place, no date, no place, remains the Orant Choir: 'Dead! dead! What a shock!'

it's Saul who transformed the rumour of the world into a funeral slab, pruned my father's century, cut out with scissors the sonorous stream of days, reduced my father's body to a gold scarab,

in the second place a box of pastries

on the other hand a box of wedding notices, much larger, likewise yellowed, written by three widows, the wedding that I might have recalled in certain dreams, if I had been born, a wedding that took place, already took place, there was no one, except the three widows, in the strictest intimacy, it's done, hurriedly behind the back of the gods, on the sly, in the presence of a large number of dead and revenants, dated, the dates flit about, frail and beautiful butterfiles, April 1936, June 1937, February 1948, the play goes quickly, the metamorphosis of the notice into for-life, of life into death, almost no time between the narrow lives, *on the other hand* a photo the tall silhouette thin narrow elegant of the young man hurried towards the exit, in the photo it's my father, Georges again, he is still alive, there we are in the street of the city, who walks at a brisk pace, a decided pace, at the end of the page the Obituary awaits him, the young man in a white suit, a belted safari jacket, he walks with a lively step, with two girls with long braids at his sides, he is holding their hands, on the right the little girl with the slender legs, girls legs from father's legs, it's the last time she advances at the rapid rhythm of the Living, as if there were all the time and space before the lively steps whereas at the end of the city street (d'Isly), She is awaiting them already, without impatience, Death, they go straight towards Her. They do not see the railing close behind their rapid progress. Still a few weeks. End of the story on this earth, but right after begins After. To be sure Destiny stole the Principal character of my Story but he returns immediately, it is he who sets the tempo all the time, the Survivor, the youngest of the whole family.

According to the Paper, the Blow had come on 12 February. What stupefaction! All of Oran shuddered. It was unexpected. To die at 39 years old: the triumph of youth.

—It's lively, says my daughter. The City takes sides for the artist of life.

—What a shock! says the Choir of Oran. Dead? Dead. Died yesterday and today deceased!

Died Thurday the 12th, on page 4, but already on the other side, on page 5, Thursday the 12th, there is the world that does not die, that talks, stirs itself, does its business, comments on its wounds and its wars, behind the back of eternity, it's the Popular Front

Fate stole my father. The guard thought he recognized the thieves. An investigation is underway.

—It's in the *Alger Républicain*, I say to my daughter.

—In all probability, thought the *Alger Républicain*, the thieves are part of that Hitlero-Vichyist gang that ruled put threat and hatred in power when I was still a seed of myself in the 40s. It brings me an unexpected comfort to learn that the *Alger Républican* would have agreed with my hypothesis, so it wasn't only from tuberculosis that my father the doctor died, it's also as a socialist and atheist that he was wounded and infected with anger and bitten to the heart by the worldwide serpent. And since the boastful publication of the Status of Jews in the *Écho d'Oran* he was fighting on several fronts, besieged in his whole being, his breath caught in pincers.

Since it was the night of 1st January, a page was turned, a large moon with a little pointed hat and a small veil was leaning high up to the left in my window. I was being watched.

If I kept a journal, it would be the journal of my death, I thought. I must confess it, confess death—to you, death! It doesn't look like that of my death. Nor that of my mother, nor that of my sweet friend.

It's a matter of the light touch of the shadow of a thought, an imaginary touch, blinking of eyelids, nonweight of a dream, passage, in the corridor that leads from sleep to waking, a shivering, silky fineness of an illusion, hypothesis with coleoptera wings—is that she? Who passes

I cannot even admit it, nor even think it, from the superfine edge of a thought, to admitting it and already she is no more. Disappeared? Remains: 'is no more'. That is not nothing. This sensation of Nomore. As if it were over. Like a dream but real. Sensation. But without. Without depth. Without face. As if it were a fault, I feel guilty of feeling, for lack of proof.

I am alive. I never doubt it. That is my strength and thus my pleasure, I trust myself. I have known many lives. I am living another one.

On one of those days, I received notice of a sentence, I wrote it down: 'I live with my death.'

I'll explain: it is suddenly the thought-sensation, certain nights, that I have received the threatening letter, and no surprise, the letter is addressed to me, not to H, a ghostly thought-sensation, that brushes up against me, only at night, and then dissipates. As soon as I rise with the day the fright evaporates, I feel nothing, reality is as usual. I attribute these moments of haunting to the excessive frequenting of the dead. Otherwise, nights are normal, with dreams. I always end up escaping from the ghosts, but is it not my doing, I am condemned and suddenly I am pardoned, at the last second, I don't know the name or the look of the last second, perhaps it doesn't exist in time, it's an invisible door.

'I live with my death': that's an assertion whose truth is intermittent. At this moment when, sovereignly, I am writing, it is empty, or else it is emptied of truth, it's fake, a discarded peel. But it happens that it bellows like a storm at sea and ineluctably I am going to drown.

When the sentence, as is the case at the moment, is but a plaything of words, it occurs to me that it is the title of my state of mind. It happens, one does everything with death, one takes meals, showers, responds to swarms of emails busy with the future, and there is no future, accompanied by a Synecdoche, which is much less sympathetic than the Syncope, the somewhat appalled, crazy even, neighbour of Kafka, a troublemaker come from the house of the Epantchines and who always seems to arrive late. My visitor has neither a hat decorated with feathers, nor long gloves, disagreeable she apes me, she sends me frightening photos in the mirror, saps me, mocks me, bites my extremities, threatens all sorts of poisons, infiltrates me betrays me apes me poisons me, instead of my cat the jackal who didn't exist is suddenly very close to me, I don't know if that quick and whistling panting is mine or its, my breathing, or its, grows shorter, with great difficulty I call the emergency medical service, but it is almost too late, midnight is too far, I don't dare wake up my daughter, 'smell that,' says the jackal, and exhales a breath of decomposition

it was the Thing which was infiltrating my body, in unknown and obscure regions, which had/has no name and no identified status either, the interior of the subject was magmatic, invaded by frightened thoughts, shivering, I felt I was affected, something dangerous was impregnating my whole organism, proposing warnings, one had a physical illness of the soul, I felt the enemy army marching invisibly towards me, I should take off, reject being buried alive, I didn't dare, I went to the slaughterhouse, to be sure the hypothesis of a fainting spell presented itself. Finally, a concrete action. In the end, H would have survived. Sitting down, crouching before the leaden sky and the dead buildings, surrounded by black spells, infected by this foreign nastiness, one wondered what is this evil

According to H, it is Death that was sending its announcements. No other explanation. According to me, I harbour the enemy Thing. I am totally incomprehensible to myself. I don't dare speak of it to anyone except to this page. People are ashamed of their terrors, that's their hold over us, by blackmail

There are events so discreet that their explosions make no noise. Suddenly one is knocked down, battered, shaken by nausea. A dream-event has just taken place. Thoughts run through the streets of my cities like they are possessed. Some think of my death. Are thrilled that she is/is not in the stairwell, on the second floor not yet/already. Mutant states, independent of my will, follow each other from one floor to the other. These are the 'humours'. 'Humours', I savour the word, they lead. I think of the term. The dead await me on the fourth floor, they are all excited. 'I'm coming!' I say. Right away, I stop. I turn. — 'It's because we're on the ship *Des Espoirs*, swell, calm, calm, swell,' the dream reminds me. 'Follow me' says the dream. As imperious as a dead king. I follow the dream. On the edge of the dream, my daughter worries, she calls me, I don't hear her.

After twenty years of suffering, it has been so many years that we no longer speak, no longer give each other life, the day came when I decided to call you, and to try to get out of this infernal silence. I was going to contest the incontestable. The décor? An enclosure in the Sorbonne. A joke, says the dream, '*je la sors bonne*', I got well out of there, as if to recall me to the limits of truth. But with regard to the little round semi-circular building like a breast of a prehistoric divinity, it was more like a pantheon. So are you going to call him? The dream and I use the familiar 'tu' form. I will call him at the end of the day, I say. Because of this perfidy on the part of the dream, I almost let the moment go by. I ponder. He was going to recognize my number, he won't answer. He had changed his number. I couldn't find his number. I was panicking. And what if I asked my daughter to do it? With her telephone. She is not crazy. Here we are, alone in this deserted building, beneath the lid of nothingness, a large colourless room, not one dead person, over there, in the corner, unique motionless presence: my computer, like a scarab. I wring my heart: to await him after so many years! He has changed, twenty years, he is angry, retiring, I would throw myself.

There I finally had a fainting spell. Afterwards, he is suddenly in the building of the 'Sorbonne', surrounded by a buzzing of neutral assistants, me in banishment. He searches for how to type a poem. He whole being is given over to the poem. This is the chance. I suggest my computer, up there in its burrow, to be helpful is without risk. A thought trembles suddenly: maybe he has someone in his life, in all this time, I had never thought of that. Oh! What a very great sorrow. Which meant that I touch his hand, I don't realize it, he doesn't run away. I touched his warm hand, the one he had given me one afternoon when we were sitting on the sofa in my bedroom, thoughtful, simple wedding in a modest and profound eternity when we were living in reality. Then I massage his whole body, I create him, I cover him in lotion, I powder him, I caress him, it is then still the living-eternity, at that moment one of the assistants becomes industrious like a bee on a flower, 'Don't touch his sex,' I say, 'it is mine.' I cannot describe the burning joy when he sets me ablaze

And then there is an explosion of barbaric sounds, inter-jections, the dream is unleashed, it seems that I have to fear the police. Where to flee? Through the bay window, one can see a narrow slope that runs outside the length of the dream.

So, no sooner found again than given back? The blaze at the moment he revives me, wakens me? There remains a violent mixture of ecstasy and pain. Can this kind of dream be avoided? It comes unannounced. And yet for days its trumpets have sounded, but softly. And those days come from distant times

When my cousin came by, it was not foreseen, neither by her nor by me. She lives in the neighbouring street, she *remem-orializes* in the same place as me, she is a lady, she wears a long floating garment of grey-coloured silk, she enters with a rustling of fabrics and papers, she drops down onto the sofa, while noting that she is putting her bottom where my mother used to sit and she exclaims: —'It has always been very high at your house.' Right away I begin hopping around like a wagtail. Since I was not on my guard, my feelings didn't have time to slip into their invisible light armour. And I found myself again with her, the lady, in the gardens of Oran around a *table tournante*, one of those tables that follow her everywhere, ever since our first floor. As usual she brings: a box of pastries to sweet talk the table and make it speak. She throws it on the table, she looks at me while blinking her eyes and she says: You have lost weight again. She has long silky white hair, long, long, that she has worn for eighty years, it's as if she looked at me with my very short hair, from all the length of her hair, and I hop about. Then the thermos having indeed fallen over on its belly—she says: ter-mo or taire-mot—, having vomited its libation, the two exfiltrated grandmothers hurried and avidly drank the spilt cocoa, each one in her way according to her kind, Omi, my German grand-mother, small, elegant, *vornehm*, conscious of her distinction, with a stylish little half-hat, the work of her milliner Frau Engers, model of modernity, with a spoon, Mémé, my monu-mental Spanish grandmother, lips drawn lapping the beverage long long black smock dress her identical archaic statue stiff slow as if in the role of hypnotic ancestor, each one her greed-iness, each one lapping up the offering of cocoa. And everywhere half-naked children hopping around. I recognized the tall slim little girl sparkling with innocence, when I was Joy-Itself, before the arrival of the fearsome Stranger. Her father had not yet taught her the word Death. And yet

From all directions the father, a tall young man with a long neck with long legs with long green eyes, more and more thin, the velvet voice came from the depths further and further away,

as if dressed in togas, less and less young, ravishing, an accelerated modern life, quick, quick, quick, on a motorcycle, duration
of a condemned one, duration of a candle condemned to melt,
on reprieve of semi-divinity, returns

The Cousin eats the cakes. They are there. Little breasts with
cream. She cannot leave them. She puts the little animals in her
mouth. There is a hunger for everything. The urge to write takes
hold of me. I feel it like a seductive hunger. If I were a painter, I
would want to lick the canvas, it's an exultation an upheaval in
her body. My Cousin cannot eat one cake. To eat one cake, one
must swallow two.

For the cats as well, desire is the soul of all the movements
of their being. As someone who is famished on a daily basis I
perceive the internal leaps of my fellow creatures, Cousins and
cats, in my body, I recognize the greedy demands, I too hear the
call of creamed cabbage and paper madeleines as soon as I pass
in front of my desk, it is very pastry-like. While I am noting this
trait on a large plate of 80-gram paper, my cat Haya arranges
herself on my tablet at the nose of my pen. Yes, if the page could
be changed into another species it would have the charms of a
living cake.

My longing is precise, just as my cat's desire for precisely
this here feather duster. What my cat loves about the (precise)
feather duster is that as soon as it is grasped, it slips away, it's
the life of the field mouse, it's not its death. What is regrettable
for the Cousin is that, unlike feather dusters and writing, cakes
are not granted the charms of flight. I don't want the feather
duster, I want to want the feather duster

The cousin eats the seventh cream puff. She can no longer stop herself. When one's back is turned, she swallows two. She is attracted by the cake. It's because she has reached the point of the vortex where the predator becomes the prey of the prey

—When I approach the point of fear, I must most urgently stop going forward, I'm afraid to reach in a moment the edge of non-return, the word fear was overtaken long ago, any minute now I am going to have lost my self, already we are in perdition in the region without route, already the hour is paralysed, time no longer advances it is the perilous state that I know, a fog spreads and swallows up aspects of the world

H. didn't know that this moment of Cousins was expected, destined to be put in the Amber of the Chamber of Memory. Since everything was happening in the incognito of a dream.

H. felt. The ghosts were small, joyous, they skipped about in the gardens, all these dead children, disguised as Indians, with puppet comrades. What is admirable about Play is that it contains worlds and all human kinds. In the Chamber of Memory, there were magic photographs that have a soul. These are small format from the 40s, which resemble memories that are perpetually young.

—Youth, there's another nymph who has disappeared from this world, don't you think? I say to the book, which follows me, accompanies me. I can still ask it the question, it is ageless, it knows what I have known. Youth: all these characters who climb, jump, embrace under the gaze of the photos are underscored by this aura. It is not an age. It's the internal light that keeps watch in a painting. The light of a vital belief. Even the dead, even those born for a short life, even my father believed in it. Even the grandmothers. The travellers come from the century without airplane. The widows too. The mountains. The palm trees. The balconies. The fresh water sellers.

It is then, around 5, around page 37 of the blue notebook, that She bit me. You don't see Her. You don't feel Her. All at once you are conquered, you are exhausted, you are expelled from Childhoods. It is Saturday, 23 January 2021, a desolate time, without struggle, without exultation, without songs without calls with melodious responses

The Cousin is eating a Cream Puff, the Cream Puff has not changed. While she eats, she is still just as young, with the cream puff all desires and all chances are revived

In Old Age, one dies very often, sometimes once a week

I knew a grandmother who lived on a pear. The pear provoked her, mesmerized her. Aroused her. A William pear. She would get up, and she would walk, heavy and irresistible, towards the attractor, she herself made me think of a William in majesty. It's not that one wants to live, it's that one wants bliss

In Youth, there is despair. When H prefers to die or to kill rather than suffer the attacks of hunger, when the heart groans and lacerates the lungs, that's the raging of Youth, a wild animal

The Cousin eats a cream puff. She doesn't eat it. She swallows it with a look. She only has eyes for the other cream puff, the cream puff after the cream puff, you don't know which cream puff will be the last cream puff,

—Poor cream puff, says my mother. Poor cream puffs.

Unlike the cream puffs, my mother is perpetual, I thought.

H. wants paper with pen. It's an appetite that is not to be questioned. I want white paper, free, without lines, rope, ramp, route, trace, an infinite piece of ponderable unknown, living, ready to leap, breathless, with pen, pen. Such is the will of my need. Each indication must be followed to the letter otherwise the spirit does not respond. This desire is such a torture. It howls, howls until the pen comes to light on the breast of the paper like the hand of the Idiot on the head of Rogozhin foaming

During the decapitation, report those who have survived this experience of such an incredible violence that afterwards one is never the same,

at the Instant of the Instant of the blade

during this Instant of which no other human being can measure exactly the immense infinitesimal duration, when

there is simultaneous double separation of the head and the body, the one and the other let one catch sight of a feeling of furious abandon, a terrible reproach from both sides, the head shoots a look of anger that is all the more appalling for being forever without successor, it assumes eternally the power over all arguments and messages that have woven the journey of a subject

Now, the unexpected feature that surges up in the Instant is that the anger of the head is directed at the body, as if it were its fault, none can deny it. It scolds the body, it barks at it, it twists its mouth in a desperate bawling out, if it could it would bite it

—Sometimes, I say to my daughter, I feel a state of decapitation. In that case I am divided, I fear the moods and the storms of my head, my body feels unjustly ill-treated. The cause of this intimate war is the stubborn recklessness of the text. It is stronger than all my elements put together.

If I could with a trembling hand caress my head, my hair, softly, the way I caress myself on the silky backs of the cats! Calm the moaning of desire! Escape myself

it is then that the Hallucinated begins to understand that one is treading a space neither floor nor ground nor route but chaotic and steep, the place of the absolute non-self, but there is no longer place, where one has to be able to call on a greater elementary force because otherwise I will never be able to come back, but there is no longer a self who could come back, the idea-of-coming-back goes away, like a dream already lost but of which one feels robbed, the secrets are lost, one no longer walks, one is walked, on the horizon, beyond all sight, perhaps an ocean could help, or an element of comparable strength to an ocean,

the violent difficulty of holding onto the imagination renders impossible any attempt at description thus at observation of the mental whirlpool, the difficulty of even just evoking the thing without being cast into the whirlpool of delirium,

these multiple and dangerous difficulties like whales in agony

one can find an echo of the groaning only in the logs of those heroes who will soon be dead for having descended into the maw of this funnel. The word 'madness' does not suffice to name the sojourn in this other reality. Only the geniuses of the descent into hell, those vulcanologists of the seas with brains formed by the ordeal of vortices, only an Edgar Allan Poe in the style of a Jonas Ramus have been able to give an account of it, but these Moseses of mental abysses pay for it when they leave. I admire them, I often meditate on their liquid tomb: it is a glacial sea, near the Lofoten islands, an opaque surface that extends farther than the eye can see, of a metallic brilliance, from which emanates a frightful respiration, a continual death rattle over kilometres, as if this element were haunted by a monster or two—that snoring is Charybdis and Scylla agonizing interminably at the bottomless bottom of an ocean. Yet the surface *pretends to be asleep* infinitely, infinitely, and it is at the end of the infinity, at the end of the stretch of metallic water, on the surface of this watchful film that an eye of the marine cyclops opens, a sort of lid rises on a sort of eye devoid of expression. Arrived here, it is a long time since words fled my tongue like sailors in a panic and I drift while stuttering

and while petrified I admire them, one hears my mother say, from another side of my brain: 'as for me, I avoid the underbrush of delirium'

—One must not see the reality of reality, it's perilous, says my son. If you knew what it was made of, you would lose it, a second would decompose infinitely, time would bleed infinitely, each thought would get lost in a thousand swirling labyrinths, you would try in vain to recount these terrifying states, the impotence of your effort to move your tongue will make words flee, a bottomless abyss would open at every hint of movement, your brain lies on its back, one cannot see this torture without tremors shaking your arms up to the shoulders soon followed by lockjaw. That is the worst —One wants to cry out, the whole book is silent

And I stayed there, in the bedroom immobilized as if on the site of an accident, buried in a lava of mutism, jaw blocked

To no longer see the sea horribly without living colour interminable jaw planted with rocky teeth moved by the shiver of a prodigiously rapid current that seems to me whipped up by unnameable furies, this whole absolutely unbearable vision, to no longer *see* the howls of a herd of monsters hidden by heavy shrouds of fog, to no longer seehear the great cries of a super-natural pain fighting in my head all of a sudden, and without my being able to do anything about it wrenching from me a shattering no: No! No! This cry booms so loud that as soon as it is out it explodes and two projectiles fall back on me

The cry of No! No! startles me: you need to keep your eyes closed. But: impossibility to keep your eyes closed.

Visual hallucinations occur on the curtains of the eye-lids. It's a tapestry of sheets of wrinkled paper bearing texts, sentences, paragraphs here and there, a word stands out, I can read it do I read it? I read it has fled, did I read it? I'm afraid of it: textual persecution. As if one could no longer stop having printed pages fill one's sight. No other horizon. Eyes stuffed with words, sentences, paragraphs. Smothering. Quick, one opens one's eyes before. Visible space returns, altogether normal. The hallucinations happen on the closed eyelids. Usually when one closes one's eyes an irregular night spreads out, slightly moving, familiar, I didn't know the point to which that night was a benediction. Instead of this naturally discreet and reassur-ing darkness, an invasion of printing. Am I going to have to live with raised eyelids, naked eyes. For how long can one bear rescue without sleeping? I am overwhelmed. I am saved by the entrance of my mother. That she now lives somewhere under the ground does not prevent her from coming. She sits down in the little armchair at the side of the bed where she is already sitting, and she begins thus:

'My dear Hélène, in my opinion you exaggerate you find yourself up there the head filled with images and a devil on your shoulders who won't let you go. As a result, you stay glued to your chair and letters accumulate on the paper like thousands of little silent birds. Too much is too much. Meanwhile I rummage about in the kitchen or take a nap while reading several books at once. *Taugenichts* by Joseph Freiherr von Eichendorff or *Le Père Goriot* by Balzac. There is also *Advice and Recipes for Difficult Times*, or *How to Live Even in Times of Need*. You must restrain yourself when it comes to paper. It would be better to go walk in the forest. One will hear real birds whistling . . .'

My mother talks from noon to four o'clock. A gentle sleep carries me off but I'm not aware of it, I don't hear the notes of her concerto, with precaution I enjoy an abundance of that internal music, that cooing sound that water emits when it returns to the dried-up bed of consciousness, my mother talkstalkstalks,

at that moment the phone rings, I say to my son.

It was an extraordinary telephone call, like the one Abraham receives on Mount Morija, in that unimaginable moment when his arm holds the knife firmly over Isaac's head, already the slightly tilted blade shivers like an eagle ready for its prey, and the arm does not tremble, a ringing of destiny, a blow, perfect in every way, in length, in details, in overabundance of love— a telephoning from the past, when you used to call me on the Amarys 100 phone when we were rich, powerful, creators of those impassioned, endless communications. Naturally *Breathers*, as you used to say Shakespeare calls us. I savoured *his accent*, I used to say my love, I adore you, I'm waiting for you, we laughed at your death, I held the vivid red phone to my mouth, to my heart, the animal was very content, I would walk in the empty rooms, on the rocks, exalted, on the shoulder of the mountain, I would traverse the palace, my innocent daughter followed me, all these elegant and deserted little rooms, I feared that you feared she would hear our hallucinated words, are you sure, the words of the dead are fragile, one doubt and it's over for the burning sighs. You would be there tomorrow, an unheard-of thing, thus there was time, the mad audacity of hope, the word *tomorrow* sparkled, yes *tomorrow* you would come, you came, you wanted, the incredible flashed, you had invoked an ordinary pretext, you would have to sign a real estate purchase agreement, it was extra-ordinarily ridiculous, there is then an administration? —I'll tell you about it, you would say. Where will we meet again? We'll see at arrival. Arrival! Such an event could no longer happen since death had struck us

everything is returned to me, everything that I had given up to forgetting

the most beautiful times of the past forever disappeared, an immense pure happiness perfect in every way, without a trace of threat, everything is returned to us: secrecy, clandestine meeting, the exaltation of managing to overcome easily all the obstacles, and right up to such a feeling of riches that I can even put an end to the felicity *provisionally* not fearing to say 'I'm going', those words that during my living life I would never have been able to pronounce, words without anxiety, 'I'm going' I say. And I don't go yet all the same. 'When you are in the plane, give me a signal' I say quickly. O the time of the signal, when we were not dead, the wink of loving time when we allowed a minimum delay in our urgency. With that: I hang up. Rash gesture, which no dream would have ever let pass. My mother is waiting for me for breakfast. She doesn't suspect for a moment that I come from Mount Morija. We talk about croissants. A golden tomorrow streams down on the scene.

Thus what is incontestably lost returns, integrally? I say to myself. On Tuesday at the heart of darkness I'm cold in a shroud of snow, Wednesday this abundance of Good.

Sitting on their stools, elegant, grace and innocence, the cats follow the events of my hallucinations on a screen in my head.

From the coast of the Lofoten Islands to the maelstrom one must go 8 kilometres swimming or in imagination, it's about the same distance as between

the fatal quay and the last steps of the ladder and the sinister thing

not the name

words are lacking but not the visions and the emotions of the self fleeing in panic,

no one and not a word to translate the terror that arises on contact of the gaze with this stretch of time sharpened over 8 kilometres of steel that follow each other by identical eternities until the vortex . . . this devil's maw that opens its eye at the end of time

—The most frightening thing, I say to my daughter, is not the hideous wink of the violent end, it is those kilometres teeming with horrors that have not yet found their Dante to tame them.

If I said: 'While traversing the kilometres of howling steel believing I saw, I saw a sea of bellowing heads,' there would be missing from this attempt at a picture the music that dislocates the order of the body and paralyses thought. Another symptom: while one makes one's way by force of an abnormal courage swimming in eight-degree water towards the eye that gapes at the end of the world, one is suddenly struck with fear upon discovering that, illusion or reality, the monster is coming towards us from the end of the world swimming at the same speed, eyes wide, inevitable, like a double attracted by its original.

At the moment that the idea I am declaring becomes clear, danger erupts like wildfire in the brain of those assassins for whom Shakespeare is the neurologist and shepherd. To have oneself for victim, for executioner, for crime and for all the actors of fate, one cannot bear it without becoming mad. Only Isaac survives up there when the trap closes.

—On the 20th, I imprudently reread Büchner's *Lenz*, I say to my son. I should not have done it, and that's why I took the book, like a potion, I made my way through the first lines, in the traces, 'On the 20th, Lenz crossed the mountain' and I followed, soon the fog came up, the air was frigid, at the beginning I felt a slight exaltation of recognition, Lenz had felt a shove in his chest, as for me in my chest I felt rather a pressure, as if a stranger's hand was gripping my heart, for the rest it was OK, it does one good to feel that one is not alone in setting off on climbing beyond reason, as for him he was looking for something but found nothing, here begins the anguish, in that sensation of nothing, as for me I was ruminating these long silences in paper, this grey fog that I feared would swallow up all the forms and figures of the book, the landscapes and especially the dreams that are like palaces, cities

how is it that the world can vanish so terribly quickly, barely had I read the first page before I felt as lost as a dream. Hard truth: for me it is time that is the problem, it is the times that are sick, for Lenz it is all the forms and volumes of the universe, all God's work that flees, there is a rent in the sky through which the stars disappear sucked into nothingness, the earth has shrunk to the point that it is nothing more than a walnut in space—I understood that I should urgently stop following Lenz, I say to my son, I had a febrile fear of contagion, this fear was already alarming. It's a fact: I am sick of time, I have great difficulties breathing, sometimes I wait for air and it doesn't come

Whence these silences, like a betrayal of my whole person, a deserted time, mummified. H. works every day but far from me, far from me, I do not write, I am thinking only of that, like the dead think, a dead thought, outside of time, without springtime, haemorrhaging like the dried-up brain of the prisoner

—I don't want to think about that, says my son, I would prefer you don't speak,

—20, I say. How to you spell that?

—54, says my son, do you know that?

—Since I was born, I have, from city to city always lived at 54 rue . . . It did no good to move

—Zeno, says my son, 54 is what paralysed Zeno. He recounts that when we take a step, in the half second that goes by between the moment we lift the foot and the moment we set it down in front of us, 54 muscles enter into play

Having learnt this by accident, he was struck down by a paralysis of his lower members. The idea of the 54 in action destroyed, in the first half second, his naive faith in God and his creation. The impression that he had forever lost his balance blew so hard around him that he fell face down on the ground. Passers-by saw in this flattening a demonstration of religious trance, but he was merely overcome by the horror of reality. To be a machine with 54,000 gears, no one can become aware of this constitution without the help of madness. Since that time, he limps

—'What relation is there between the muscles of walking and the staircase of my house?' but I didn't have time to *pose* this question, the half second had gone by since an interminable half second

Likewise: Suddenly traversed by a great shudder Isha my cat throws herself on Haya my cat with the aim of slitting her throat, casting her out of the universe, erasing afterwards any trace of the passage of her twin and her other self on earth, pushing into the crater of nothingness the cadaver of her sister-self.

Likewise: The homicidal shudder swirls already deep in the throat of the hallucination, between Abraham and son growl fits of indomitable rage, wild looks are unleashed from one face to the other like a pack of howling demons

Likewise between my son and me stands the Shadow, we feel frightfully threatened, an offensive is being readied, nightmares set up everywhere in my head senseless quarters, dwellings with neither head nor tail, bodies of immense and emptied buildings like hollow mountains, a world of delirious distances and without exit, and everyone seeks and cannot find an elevator a stairway that does not lead to an interior wall

To whom can I describe the 'innocent' air of the visitors to my house this night—a kitchen knife of a threatening length, not less than a metre, with a wide blade, and thereupon 'the man' asks for a whetstone, he has a face that is barely disguised, and I act as if it were banal, as if it needn't alarm me, I needn't make note of it in my notebook, as if I hadn't recently reread the last chapter of *The Last Day of a Condemned Man*, as if at the end of this page it would be *Four O'Clock*

This is how it happens that one lets oneself drown in the blink of an eye, sleepwalking.

Thereupon to my astonishment I read Woolf's journal as if it didn't annoy me, didn't make me shiver with a sort of frightened disapproval

all this force and these gifts so as to celebrate the cult of her immortal morbidity. The crowned migraine. And for the first time I follow her condemned one's haste. She has just read. 'It is a quarter after one,' here is what we feel now, the condemned one, thus the author of the Journal of the writer Virginia Woolf, thus me, despite my efforts to keep from being dragged into the swirling abyss: —a violent stranglehold on the head by a circle of iron or steel, an eruption of despair, that is, of frozen expectation, the terrible pain of a dead one who still suffers, every time I stand up or lean over, there is a liquid that makes my brain beat against the walls of my skull, a swarm of terrified ants around the hippocampus, I have cramps that feel like they could break my tibias and my eyes burn and howl at the fire.

'Two hours and forty-five minutes more, and I will be cured,' she reads. How many dozens of agonies before arriving at the cure she thinks, how long death is. It's not that she takes herself to be him. She *is* him.

For the first time, in reality, I am what I flee.

It is two o'clock, judging by the black night of page 50, I will not be surprised to be awakened by a telephone call. Was

I sleeping? Was I dreaming? I was observing the cloth stretched across the internal surface of my eyelids. It was a wrinkled white fabric, of which I could admire the cleanliness and subtlety of its whiteness without feeling anything other than an aesthetic satisfaction. An immensity that having done its work of folds and traces was now calm like a sea of cloth. Such an infinite living and silent stretch like God at rest after creation and under my little eyelids. Soon after, the fabric having disappeared without my being able to be warned of its disappearance it is an infinite calm blue sky that stretched out, under my 4 cen-timetres of eyelids. And then this whole sweet contemplation is pierced like a retina by a phone call. While I transcribe describe this faithfully, for this moment is engraved imperishably on one of my mental pages, I still hear the cry of the telephone: an abominable, lugubrious croaking, and not at all natural, that I cannot even compare to the creaking of one of Poe's ravens, for the *Ravens* of this poet are imaginary birds—if they are birds—automatons marvellously imitating the worst crows whose unpleasant chattering everyone has heard in actuality. There, this croaking had such a savage sound, so against nature, but real, like the voice of a large knife held against a whetstone, that to give the shadow of an idea of it, the impression of fear and incredulity that I felt, I can connect it only to that of an unfor-tunate friend of James Hogg, when during a solitary walk he hears his name called by none other than Satan. To come back to the phone call, by comparison, I had just gone from the celes-tial to the infernal.

—William Wilson on the phone, croaks the Voice.

Before the end of the second, guided by an electric reflex, I had hung up the way one draws one's hand back from a furnace

Those who have crossed on their human path this emperor of monsters will understand me.

Those who have never had to draw their hand back from a furnace at supernatural speed, warned by these lines, can venture at the risk of the demon. A double demon, on the job. He, and William Wilson his disgusting double, have no more left Oxford than an assassin his crime or than a crime its author.

—It's Hell, I say to my daughter. Poor old word!

I wanted to paint the horror, 'hell' is the only precise and correct word than I can grasp in the language and it was all dried up. A lexicalized metaphor! Like the mummified cat in the closet. Dull, gloomy word. I wished I was able to throw it furiously far from me, let it go, stumble against the wall like the William Wilson despised by William Wilson himself. Neither Dante nor Poe could revive those mortal remains. Dostoevsky, perhaps. But at the cost of what fits of madness? I say to myself: for someone who is mad about language not to be able to paint Hell in words is Hell. Or Shakespeare's solution: decapitate the language of Lavinia, but no poet can go to the end of the paradox of Abraham the mute: to no longer express oneself except in the Inaudible of God, this language that makes itself understood only by the bone's marrow. Or Celan's solution, the agonizing struggle of sentences, the stuttering of the subject, fragments of broken thoughts, scattered

It's like the word 'Terror'. Here's one that instils a fear as intense, as near as the one that erupted when we were in our childhood bedroom and, backed against the wall of the night, we couldn't flee the ogre who came at us as calmly as the portly old man with the red, pimply face who buried the Condemned Man in the sleeves of his jacket with the impassive skill of a butcher busy with his carcass

and no one knows what makes for the power of this phenomenon of mental hurricane. There are outbursts of internal and nearby howls, turmoils of images. You are looking at the main alley that leads to the gate while winding between the trees, in truth you don't *look*, you let your gaze wander over this familiar path, it is then, without any warning sign, without a cloud, without a cause, without anything, there, in front of your eyes, a trembling at first slight then more and more accentuated grabs hold of this long body, this serpent of flagstones and mosses that obviously is your mortal enemy. But the path has nothing to do with it. This frightful reaction is produced by the contact of the gaze and the usually inanimate form. A perverse, treacherous divinity totally indifferent to human fate, perhaps without will and without reason, is behind this action that causes the feeble human construction to derail. With a large shiver the targeted subject quickly turns its head aside, it's a healthy reflex. But sometimes, as in the case of the Condemned Man, who wanted to turn his head, at quarter after three thus forty-five atrociously long brief minutes before the sound of the steps of the last minute in the staircase—sometimes the body does not want to, the nape remains paralysed, and 'as if dead in advance' testifies Hugo, and everything is already coming apart.

—I can no longer look at the alley, I say to my son.

—I don't wish to hear talk about the neck—says my son.

—'Have pity!' cries the Condemned Man. 'One minute to await my pardon, or I'll bite!' I say.

Those words, says my son, are ejaculated in a gargle of blood, by the head. And the body twists, for its part.

—The terror is the terror of being a prisoner *in* the Thing, says my son. The bitter sap of terror is the state of being kept outside of oneself in the debauchery of hallucinations

—When I was in the Thing, I say, I was not even scared. Hours went by, one episode after another, without stopping. Once, around 3.30, I was also in 'Afganistan', my head still reeling after the speech I had just given. Alone in this deserted landscape, ochre-coloured, a scattering of rocks, no road or streets, I was going towards a likewise disorderly, yellowish horizon. On my side, the other side, I was filing my papers in a folder. The only identifiable feature was the name 'Afganistan'. So I knew where I was, 'Afghanistan' is like this. My brain over-flowed from one place to another.

It would have no end. A state of metaphor

Around four o'clock, I felt a panic forming like a tornado, I called my doctor. I don't know if I said 'I am in Afganistan' or if I specified 'Afganistan without H'. That is to say, without me. I was in the country without me

III

MDEILMM

MOLE SPEECH

It was the Saturday of Easter —Tell me, my doctor was saying to me.

I was making an Impossible Crossing. I was no longer waking up: I was in an Imaginary Story. I said 'you' to myself: 'You are in an imaginary story, worse still: in an imaginary *dream*.' I wasn't dreaming, I was in my bedroom, I didn't see how to get out of it, since I had lost time. I say to my daughter: 'I am blocked in a hallucinating hallucination.' 'You seem perfectly normal to me,' says my daughter. I was stopped at page 17. The next page I was at page 17. There was no other next page. The bedroom also no longer moved. 'There are very specific things,' I say to my daughter. 'A bizarre temporality, foggy, disappeared.' I was waiting for this problem to vanish. This unspeakable accident happened at three o'clock. A kidnapping of the world. Or else it's a confinement in an unshakeable illusion. No doubt I am deprived of my rights and my will. Forbidden. I believe it is temporary. This is a sign that I have a superpowerful brain outside the confining bedroom. The Hallucination, I say to myself, is, without question, part of reality. What tells me that this reality is a hallucination of reality is that this reality, unlike reality, evaporates after some immaterial time, dissipates, to be followed right away by another epoch. Then I remain successively in the tunnel as if I were going for whole days in two superimposed trains. Not as if. I am in two realities, the one is more colourful than the other, the other is a little 'out of date', tenuous, but sincere, truthful. It is this slight paleness that leads me to call it 'the other'. But perhaps the other is not the other of the one. Yet it is in the so-called one that I feel the most acute anxiety and this state of shameful strangeness that incites me to phone people close to me, supposing that they are in a reality. I add that these twin realities where I am alone are joined and simultaneous. I am myself there.

I was on the other side. I was saying to myself: what if I don't come back. More precisely: 'If I don't come back. Make my will.' I note down hastily without difficulty but precipitously for fear that this capacity to join sentences and to form words on paper will be confiscated from one second to the next. Every half second counts. This will had three different lines, imperative and abbreviated. I have misplaced it. Misplaced is not the word. It left. That's because it was part of the hallucination. It began thus: 'If something happens to me'

'Something' was written in quotation marks. I didn't know who or what this 'Something' was. It was 'the worst'. I used words like pokers to stir the embers. 'The worst' is not death. One will never know

Then I set down the shortest words, I went for monosyllables, shortcuts, and reaching the signature I signed with my initials, all of this is well traced

It is the history of the Stolen Will.

—Tell me, my doctor was saying to me.

Right away I felt the duty to tell. The words would encircle the second reality and rein in it. I was convinced of that. I want to tell what has just happened, a minute ago, what has just happened there, my tongue is ready, what happens, I put forward a word, instantly it takes off, it frays, it's still there, just in front of me, I start over. A word comes forward and leaps away in the opposite direction. It's ungraspable, it goes too quickly, it's gone, like a dream that leaves,

For hours, in vain

—When I was mad, says my son, I saw everything, I could recount everything but there was no I.

—At the moment I was going to give an account, I say, I began, I think I can put forward a word, and there's nothing more. A little perceptible something, foggy. I was surprised. Had I lived what I had just lived? Where am I? Was I?

I tried, I didn't want to disappoint whoever came to my aid

I came back. How? As I had left, without prologue or conclusion,

I was in reality, and during this time I was in the other reality. The latter didn't have the same substance but it was indeed I who spoke when I spoke. I was not mad since I was in the reality of the realities. Only it was exhausting, I was shrinking, there was a melting of my wits I was turning pale, in the lefthand reality

—What is surprising is the duration.

—For hours. What is surprising is that I knew the time. The same in the two rooms. It is working for two that is exhausting.

In a certain way it is very funny. In a same certain way it is as terrifying as being buried alive in two joined graves. You get worn down

—So just like that you went into quirkiness.

—I didn't 'go', I found myself abandoned there. Not having gone there I didn't know how to come back. I lacked for everything

The exit can come only from the outside.

It is useless to hope or to despair. The one Condemned to death will be cured in two hours. 'Cured'. There is a word that delighted him, it is as if he had come upon a secret hidden behind the language. What delights him makes him tremble: when one speaks, the language says all the words in another simultaneous language, two messages are launched in the same breath in two equal and different directions, one doesn't choose, one doesn't decide, one forks, one is forked, one is what one thinks one says something other than what one thinks one says. Someone will be gay, someone will have laughed, the Question posed to the Condemned one is frightfully destabilizing: if, dead, I come back, what do I, from now on two, choose to be my ghost, is it the head or the body? The man—one of the selfs of the Condemned one—has sore elbows. Now that is an odd symptom, I say to myself. It sometimes happens that the soul is lodged in the elbows, my poet says. For another it is lodged in the feet. My dog Fips had his soul in his heart, I saw it beat in his chest, he was a fool for love. I have forgotten him

The 20th at four-thirty I found myself back in the confusion of the Room of Sorrows. What a journey! How I had forgotten it. It's the room where my dead and my terrors sleep. You can hear my voice bewail its fate: I am alone, alone sounds my lone breathing, it is Psyche who whispers. My voice pours out from the hollow of my right hand: I suffer from solitudes, all my friends are dead, but my fingers still live, a need for paper animates them, thirst to caress their silky spine. All my friends have left. How I have forgotten them. Forgettings accompany my Solitude. My Solitude takes speech, strangles it, shakes it, tears from it a sob that it smothers. It was going to say: I suffer from you. Time barks

At night I'm afraid, during the day I'm cold, the French language makes me laugh, because of it I have what I do not have. There is something comical in the Company of the Other, when one is simultaneously in two adjacent realities. It's as if I had an internal roommate. But it is I, and not my chatty roommate, who am attacked, it seems to me. It is I who am, I who have, I who calls,

The voices that answered me, the voices that nourished me with the music of life are lying down, I can't disturb them. Shivers run under my forehead, my jaws are petrified, my body is laughing at me. My life no longer has any friends. A country that I had loved, where I had rejoined my dear friend, having faith in eternity, has just tipped over into a frozen nothingness, I read this in the Newspaper of one of the Realities. I am sitting on the little sofa like an escapee, Terror in the armchair that faces me. It announces to me that Life is going away, is going far away, is going away for a long time and forever, it doesn't announce it, it knocks quickly, with a rap on the back of the heart. The heart leaps, begins to gallop, froths, runs, runs, until exhaustion. It's the roof of the house that a gust of wind has torn off.

Afterwards I forget. I leave the Room of Sorrows without turning around. I have forgotten. It's that one cannot not forget that today at three o'clock we lost the roof of the house, the skull confidence, Maman's shoulder, the beloved's hand

I came back around seven o'clock. There has been an exit. 'Cured'. As if by a dream. But it was by reality. One has come back to oneself. Afterwards one often shudders. The terror is never far away. What is marvellous with the Hallucinations is their way of evading. They reign they flee, unnoticed, one cannot grab onto them. They are totally foreign divinities. Certain people adore them. I have a horror of them. They are prisons. After they dissipate, they leave the legs weak a fatigue weighs on the whole bodily space. I don't understand how this blow that was struck was taken back

Who wants to prevent us from keeping the keys to the other side One would like all the same to draw some bitter pleasure from these frights

If I do not regret this time of terror, I want to dread it. But already yesterday is so far, so diminished, so doubtful, I have just written the date: 4 April 2021. So a year has passed since last week? Time slips by under our noses at very great speed, at the end of this very line it is already 4 December, life and death devour each other

Between the 5th and 6th of April and without explanation there are Nights of Grace. Because one was not expecting Perfect Graces, Graces where there were Resurrections

We were like the Lost Ones of Life, on the point of moving into a slaughterhouse. A dog was howling like mad at death. If the heart could howl like a dog, it would help us. Abraham's heart bellowed for no one. So it's Easter?! We are resuscitated. It happens. It has happened to me three times in forty years. And yet I was really dead and lacked all hope, and all of life was on the side of my beloved. I adapted to these circumstances of scarcity, like Kafka adapted to being structurally a prisoner, one cannot say that in this state the soul takes place, it has no place, it simmers, it takes non-place, it is outside and there is no inside, nor ocean, nor music and even suffering does not make one suffer, since it is more than difficult for me to describe that state of selfwidowhood, I will stop, I am beaten down

Now it happens that from this exhaustion a spark flashes and a dead seed gives birth to a rosebush. That is God. Next, and lastly, me,

I am writing this in human time it is not I who am dead, the soul accepts to occupy my body without being asked to do so, because from my study all my senses give onto the universe. I do not command. I state.

In April 2021, there were the Resurrections. It was the 14th of that month. Why that day precisely? Omi my grandmother was born 14 April 1882, but according to me that is not it. The 14th of April was free of any traces, it seems to me. That day and not another, he came back, my dog protector. But who came back? Who is in the garden, at the end of the strange alley? It took me as long to go from the unbelievable to the believable as it took Hamlet to go from the Illusion to the ghost of his king in person. Who is standing, a dog deposited living totally motionless sculpted in a brilliant form fawn-coloured, patient as an angel. Fips! I cried. He has come back?! It has been seventy years since I last saw him in the garden. My dog protector. Suddenly he was there as heartbreaking as Cathy in the mystical night of *Wuthering Heights*, but in the middle of the day, real, o his little body, like a perfect hallucination, ideal. I cried. Fips! I was drunk. Fips! I was on the threshold of all-house. He was there, immobile, in the middle of the garden, waiting. Between us the space lightly ripples. I cried: Fips! I ran. I was on my knees in front of him. His ears folded down over his eyebrows! Everything was love. His eyes. He had a large white spot on his chest. So it wasn't really Fips? Not altogether Fips. It was another Fips. I was convinced of it. That doesn't prevent Fips. In seventy years, I will have a white spot on my chest. Fips, I say. He didn't run away. I want to believe it is Fips. I believe. I hug him. What emotion. Nothing prevents Fips having appeared perfectly present, real, for a few moments. He was an envoy.

The First Revenant. Until that day I had never thought of a return of Fips.

This event took on a growing importance, as if this scene was going to change my life.

—You know Fips? I say to my daughter. What do you think of him?

—He's a character in your fiction, says my daughter, I know about his suffering and his disgrace. I think he was not a pretty dog. He was a barker. He couldn't defend himself while doing his own apology.

—Fips, I say, is a fighter, a disarmed gladiator. Fips dies young. I must write the passion according to Fips. Fips fell like a soldier, out of mad love for a tiny nation. Muscular, elegant, of a small size, rapid as a leopard, formed in fawn-coloured skin, Fips, I say, is the descendant of Argos and the spiritual son of my father. In the *Alger Républicain*, it was said: 'Hitlero-Vichyist racism is not unrelated to this premature death'

—But who gave that ugly name to this noble spirit? Fips, pss! pf! sp! There's an onomatopoeia that does not elevate the person thereby named. Spif! ps!

—Perhaps my mother, the namer, found in this name the superior and mythological powers that Felicity felt carried Loulou off to the side of the Holy Spirit?

—I didn't know he had come back, says my daughter

I had said nothing about it, before now, even to myself, the way one keeps secret an event whose grandeur surpasses us, fearing to do it harm, to diminish it, with an awkward word. I had consigned it to a silence like the one into which Coleridge cast his most colossal hallucinations. When one has seen God or one of his substitutes, one instinctively secures the treasure with an absolute discretion.

This had never happened. I wept over it internally. Just once, to love him at last totally. To say to him: There is only one dog, and the Unique one is you. I have never loved anyone but you.

Those are the very words that I say in all fervour and truth to the Beloved.

It was Easter. Almost all my friends were dead. Having no more lives I was going to move in with my brother. With one ear I heard flow by the morning bird songs, one can survive with this invisible music. With my left ear I heard Fips barking far away, a ghost of barking, which doesn't console but reassures. Suddenly you appeared. A little impromptu visit. Everything being over between us, I was not prepared. You had withdrawn. You were dead, that was a fact. So my mother was wrong: that a dead one comes to visit, for her that was de la *foutaise*, bullshit. She loved this French word, *foutaise*, a slight erotic vibration, something secretly animal. My mother never had any intention to come back. —Leave me alone with your devilry. When it's over it's over. —But what does that mean, over? —What's the point of your going to the cemetery to talk to bones?

You were coming to see my lodging. It's a large concrete building, still empty. As you approached, at about 3 metres, fire burst out in my being, then you were before me. I contemplated your face. Desire burned. You were near me, standing, near the table. I was as motionless as motionless Fips in the middle of the garden. Such an event is so fragile. We had a conversation. The words flowed gently, I don't remember them, I had such an ancient thirst I drank. My hand, oh! I look at it, without my being able to stop it, is madly attracted by your sex. It's by chance and magnetism that I touch it lightly. And there, you do not withdraw. The table holds its breath.

It was Sunday, 22 January 1854, it was nine-thirty in the evening in Jersey. And Hugo lightly touched Shakespeare's sex. They touched each other's souls in French. And they used the familiar form of address. I raise my eyes. It's a daring gesture.

Oh! Your eyes! Your eyes of an impassioned king. You want yes I want. We want. The scene was happening between our physical souls. Already our lips. Let us not doubt. Our souls laugh. Would a life be possible like this, sometimes, perhaps stronger than anything. The table moves. It's my brother no doubt who sees us. Shakespeare seems tense. 'Speak!' says Hugo

—'Mdeilmm.'

It's the first time I hear a word in ghost. I'm not sure I'm writing it correctly. 'Leave', I say to my brother, 'leave please, go eat something!' I plead: a half-hour! I push him towards the door. Forty minutes! I beg. I am not a beggar. I would give a life for each minute. Shakespeare knows it. I am asking my brother for life. I owe him an explanation.

—You know that Hugo speaks with Shakespeare? You know what he says to him? Shakespeare?

—Remember me?

—No. He says: Mdeilmm

—'Name?' says my brother. —No, I say: Mdeilmm. —Madam? —No, I say: Mdeilmm. —I don't get it! Never heard this word. It's your invention? —Shakespeare's. Leave quickly, leave! I'm afraid that death will come back.

I should close the door, lock it. Already our lips, how they join half-opened like answered prayers, it's enough to faint from sweetness, this Act IV of *Antony and Cleopatra* can last fifteen eternal scenes. Antony, You have Returned, live die / No force in the world could achieve this Return. I repeat the Shibboleth: 'Mdeilmm.'

I am a specialist in Revenants. I should call this book: *Mdeilmm*. This idea enchants me. It is just and noble. I end by giving into it and propose it to my editor.

—The word shows off, sparkles, admirable Shakespeare! In one sole breath half-snorted half-whispered, it 'says' very well the difficulty be it only in evoking *Encounters with Our Revenants*, the Winds that blow up there on the passages of the ramparts, the cliffs that sway on their base, the pack of waves that snarl and salivate in the lion pit

and all the spiritual outbursts that terrify the natural world when a *Traveller* from Foreign Lands crosses again over the border, the problems with the Visa, the obligation to wear a visor, the indecipherable guards in front of the closed gates, the candidates who grow old standing for a long time at the threshold while waiting for permission, the shapeless crowd of the bloodthirsty who trample one another and would decapitate one another if they had bodies to assuage their urges, and somewhere, in the middle of the sorrows and regrets, a garden, the size of a modest paradise and tailored for two persons, filled with thick lavender and rosemary bushes that form cushions for our heads, and totally protected from the universe of terrors, I was saying —and what is precious, I was saying, is that it is unique and inappropriable. Md . . .

—The problem, says the editor, is that one can't pronounce it. —My editor reflects. Is it a word? A proper name? —Prudent. Hospitable. —A migrant? There are so many words come from so many languages in transit through the French language. Or one of those vestiges of a religion whose gods didn't last long? Does one pronounce each letter one after the other? —It is

pronounced in one breath, I say, it is just one syllable. Mdeilmm.
—An intruder, something Artaud spat out, one never knows.
It's perhaps a key found in a bottle of Edgar Poe's. The stuttering
of a dream?

—How did That come to you, how came to you That?

—It came to Victor Hugo, I say

I say the truth. One will note: in this ordeal, my editor will
proceed with the precautions of a cat in the labyrinth of a fable,
step by step, flat on the ground, detecting, practising a wise indecision. Who knows in what fabulous field he might find himself
caught. My editor is not mad, he is accomplished. As an ambassador of madmen and defender of the lost, he takes care not to
fall off the edge of the cliff into the chasm of fictions. The inde-
terminate and unnameable things and whatevers about which
you don't know if they are mined or *inaminate*, he puts them
under observation, he tests them from a distance with the help
of prudent and respectful words. And he waits. A heavy security
door is half-opened by someone passing by, over there at the
back of the stage,

As for me, at the sight of this gap through which the judges
and executioners are going to surge, I would yell: No! No! He
maintains his tone, not the least annoyance.

—My little problem, says my editor attenuating, will surely
be with the G.d (for what begins with *G* and ends with *d*, perhaps Grand or God) and The Commercial side. You will surely
have readers. One cannot ask a reader to *retain* the Md-word,
that is the only thing that bothers me, I go into a bookstore and
I cannot say 'Do you have Mmmm? —It begins with M, I say.

I explain myself.

—I like Mdeilmm. Mdeilmm is not a neurological accident. Mdeilmm existed. One could compare Mdeilmm to a meteorite, Mdeilmm has crossed one of my supranatural nights, like a little shining star in my darkness. In its trajectory this little celestial body emitted a music of the spheres.

—It resonates perfectly with what you —? says the Defender

—It's Shakespeare who said It to Victor Hugo, says Hugo. It was a January evening, in Jersey. Mdeilmm. The transtemporal telephone the two were using was a little round table set on a square table, it's the little one that spoke. The language of communication, in this case, was French.

Four trustworthy witnesses were present when Shakespeare said Mdeilmm to Hugo. According to them, Md. Md. was not a code, rather it was a spontaneous interjection and like the sound of a collision between two languages, but the etymology remains uncertain. One may wish to think that the apparent bizarreness of this word, neither altogether French nor certainly English, would be explained by the fanciful quality of Shakespeare's French as one may see in *Henry V*.

—How to explain, I say to my son, that the undeniable resistance posed by this word —if it's-a-word —to assimilation by the ordinary users that we are, does not at all trouble the four interlocutors? Three men and a woman and no one around the table asks: How do you spell 'that'? That no one asks the question of the choice of language strikes me, but the four guests seem to be unaffected by any hesitation, they express themselves *in some language*. This language stands for any language. Whence the facility with which it accommodates a great diversity of formations. Moreover, they are not just anyone whose super-abundant remarks are noted down simultaneously by the stenographer assisting them. One also senses that the master of ceremonies doesn't miss a drop of this continuous stream, not out of avarice but as if he feared the consequences of a natural interruption: this rhythm, this hurried and regular pace of the interrogations, these articulated replies, this occasional terseness, everything tells us that it's not a matter there of a simple conversation, but of an exchange that obeys strict implicit rules, as it would be in a laboratory experiment. Thus when Shakespeare lets drop or spits out or expectorates this word-if-it-is-a-word with great force, a sonorous object whose vibrations promise to be incalculable, no one dares to express the least sign of curiosity or strangeness. —It's as if he had sneezed. For centuries, true Shakespearian actors are recognized as those who perform the sneezes of Polonius, recognizable among all others and so fateful since they are the cause of his death when they betray his presence behind the curtain, as if they were inhabited by the spirit of Polonius. But it is not a sneeze.

Afterwards, according to the little round table, Shakespeare, the one *who is there*, will proclaim in verse the near-nothingness of human masterpieces, compared to the Unique Total Work engendered by the God of Eternity *on the basis of a single word*. According to the round table, Hugo too is concerned by this merciless assertion. And reciprocally, thinks Hugo, I say to myself.

According to me, if the little round table reports a dialogue that surpasses all of us, as for the square table, it says not a word. It has its doubts. It has its feet on the ground like my mother.

Shakespeare also doubted everything, all speaking, thinking, desiring-fearing beings. It occurs to me that the little round table is perhaps the one that my Aunt Deborah bought in 1928 in a second-hand store reserved for the initiates of Oran when the sale was held of the talking objects and sophic furniture of Madame Leonetti, the most secretly renowned theosophist of that philosophical city, at whose home the faithful went once during her weeks up until the last one. People used to say of Madame Leonetti that she had had with Victor Hugo the honour that Mademoiselle de Gournay had with Montaigne, as she herself used to say.

This idea has so much charm that I 'see' for a moment Deborah's pedestal table, when it would sway under the influence of the spirit of her doctor-brother, my father, she said, coming on purpose even dead to write a homeopathic prescription for her, or for anti-rheumatism cream.

It is impossible that this pedestal table is Victor Hugo's round table. Deborah's pedestal table has only one foot. If this foot was raised it would fall down. Here it is my mother herself who intervenes among us. It must be the evocation of my Aunt Deborah that causes her entrance into the scene, and probably her spirit, which was always avid for rhyming, does not resist the expression 'Deborah's-pedestal-table', that is '*guéridon-de-Deborah*'. A treat for her joking spirit, that she got on the one hand from her husband the doctor who everyone said had the gift (*don*) to have cured (*guéri*) everyone but himself, my father the prince of deadpan humour (he was a *pince-sans-rire* to recall another expression that belongs to the treasury of family wit), on the other hand from the vast German lineage versed in *Witz* from generation to generation, since the passage of Napoleon called *Bohne Apart* by the great-aunt of my grandmother Ilse Meyer, who was passing through Jena, precisely.

—So let's set aside the pedestal table, I say, and let's come back to the medium by which Shakespeare addresses Hugo. In question is a round table with eleven feet. Round and rare, this table as a telephone able to abolish distance and time can transport speech instantaneously only if one *asks* it to please respond to the pressures of the several legs that rub and bounce between its feet. For the spirit, which has no force, to be able to start the table working physical and spiritual muscles have to be mobilised. One cannot say that it is the table itself that speaks of its own accord: but it is indeed the table that lends its wooden body to the spirits that are burning to meet each other, whether the souls reside with the living or with the dead. Because of this question of feet, one could not speak to one another alone in a tête-à-tête.

—'Who is there?' With those words begins the interrogation of the table. The brusqueness of Hugo's tone can be interpreted several ways. Does he sense that this table that looks like a table is nothing other than the wooden body in which Shakespeare is preparing to be recognized? Are there in the piece of furniture promises of divine revelation, perhaps in the grain of the wood? One would have to know in what kind of wood, with what logs, descendants of what ancient forest, comes this form, it's the whole anatomy and archaeology of worlds that are kept in this animated inanimate body, this chest of secrets. For if Hugo has the urge to say these words among all possible words, it's because it's the table, that is to say, the borrowed body, that whispers them to him. Those three words are as vital and familiar for the interested party as the key that opens the tragedy of *Hamlet*. It's as if the table had given Hugo a kick. *'Someone'* would have given Hugo a kick. 'Someone' is an aspect, not altogether human, a memory activated of a person, he or she, who was adored feared adorfeared.

If it was I who mmurmured, I would say *'Who's there?'*, since English was our secret language, and if it was my brother or Fips my dog brother, we would say, 'It's You, Papa?' knowing that my father the doctor always knew the art of making unexpected apparitions in various costumes of revenants. More than once my 'father' rushed by in front of a door wearing a richly coloured uniform, coming from upper worlds and I didn't recognize him. It's only long after that a voice said to me: that character who passed like lightning like a supernatural postman dressed in purple, some emperor, that actor trimmed all over in gold who stuck his head crowned with a golden cap through the front door, that was your—

And I was terribly sorry like Perceval, afflicted, bereaved and subject to the harsh law of revenance: He Returned, and He can return only on condition that no one say his name and silence is maintained. Yet it was always the same someone who crosses my sight, coming from my right, at great speed, and, I note, stretched out like a angel swimming on the wings of dream, to disappear in the direction of the garden. And I would never see his face.

According to the book, one sees thereby that 'my-father' did his training as a young transdoctor destined to a precocious future of a ghost.

To think that all will have begun with the fear and nervousness of the officer Bernardo, a battle-tested soldier who is sensitive to the presence of invisible powers. We will see him in a minute. He bristles like my cat warned before I am of the ghost walking in the alley. *Who's there?* First and last question. What a question! How it trembles with the fearful desire of the living for those scouts from the beyond, those pioneers of unimaginable countries. The dead, who are nothing without us, are our masters

First one hears his voice

Before everyone and all the time one hears his voice, that of the first man before humanity, all trembling and sweaty launch itself towards the Unknown, the darkness in front of him moves and he doesn't know who is to be born from this howling nothingness. To be born is not to be, it is to make the acquaintance of infinite fragility. So he barks, his throat anxious, the first word of the world and it's a sigh: *Who?* Who?

—Bernardo, the one who takes the first human step on the tragic planet, the first atom, prehistoric man, the ancestor of the Anxious. He doesn't know who he is, who you are, who I am, and any animate presence threatens him, he is himself his own hostility. He is haunted.

—'No. Not like that.'

—Who is speaking there? I say to myself.

—I had just written those three words. 'He is haunted'

—No, not haunted, says the paper. At the moment my pen raised its nib, a voice scolds me: Not haunted, not *hanté*, repeats the paper. *Enté*, grafted. You'd think you were dreaming. And yet if the table talks why not the paper? The page, this long mirror in which slumber my pending thoughts and my self-portraits. When I am in front of its blank, its enigmatic length, am I not in the same state as Bernardo before the black page, I lean over it, I am dizzy, I feel there is reason and I don't know who is going slowly to take shape on the surface?

And Shakespeare gives the word. And this word is not any of those collected in *Shakespeare Glossary* by C.T. Onions. No one knows who creates this word. It is a unique word. Hugo says that it's Shakespeare who says it. Or else it's Shakespeare who says what Hugo thinks he says. *He*, no one knows who that is, there. Who created whom and what? Does there exist another word as unique as the word Mdeilmm? This word, this unique word, is it? At the beginning he says nothing. Shakespeare or Hugo says this object for use one time, one of the two of them, the other repeats it, and once repeated the word thing becomes a word.

—I want to speak about it but I notice that I cannot speak it, I say, it makes me speak.

The next day I decide to send the thing become-word spelt out to my son. It's an experiment. The word arrives in silence and in letters to the addressee.

I'm counting on the fact that my son as a mathematician is an expert in formulas that are indecipherable for the ignorant but recognized by the learned.

—Suddenly, I don't see clearly. I know MDR and PTDR but that is not it, I am Mdmourning. It says nothing to me. If it's the title of your book, I will tell you if I like it when I have read it, I go into a bookstore, and one hears a funny sound, a mouse's mmm, an eileileil, one would think it's the voice of Josephine the singer, deceased in 1923 and set out to dry between two volumes of Kafka's fables, says my son

—The poor little one! says my mother who hears (thinks she hears) 'a passed person' moaning under a gag

—One feels it's a suitcase word, says my son, but I'm having trouble opening the suitcase. Would it be Gaelic? It's a Yiddish word!

—And what if it were the last word of a language that is disappearing? Already the mouth is full of dirt, like all Breathers, the tongue moves and calls mmama, my daughter thinks

—This word was pronounced one time. We know, because it was taken down by Auguste Vacquerie, the nonbeliever, the advocate of truth. Here is a man who remained unconvinced so long as the table expressed itself like an ingenious lady. It's only when, having changed the table three times, the last little one ends up emitting a squeak, I say, so Hugo,

—but I'm getting lost, and I feel in my mental chamber, which is also my study, the passage of eminent and cherished presences, sometimes crossbred, in the space of my head they rub shoulders in the same time to the point that I confuse them, is that ironic look that cough, that juggling of words and sighs my father or Kafka?

—It's in *The Last Day of a Condemned Man*, suggests my son, step by step in the darkness, list ô list: Mdeilmm! But it's the sound the guillotine pronounces when falling with its whole blade!

—But Hugo says that it's Shakespeare who says mdeilmm to Hugo and Hugo is a great trickster, says my daughter. He invented it

—To invent such a word, that's genius, I say to myself. There was inspiration by table. Hugo believes and thus feels, or feels and thus believes that he is Shakespearized. One has to be a great alchemist to defy the rules of spelling and pin vertigos on the tip of letters. Mdeilmm is the result of a Hugolysis.

This word makes us speak. It moves. It provokes, jostles. It's disequilibrium. I vacillate. For a while Hugo is bewitched by his marionette. It happens. When one is bewitched one doesn't know one is bewitched. One bewitches oneself. One word is enough. The word casts a spell over its speaker. The speaker thinks they think. They think, they do not think. The word moves about on the table. It makes things move. Mdeilmm takes me for a ride. It is off-balance. I write off-balance. Out of dis-equilibrium. I rely on a great number of different people, so many feet and looks, it is is what pushes me, makes me go on makes me dizzy.

When 'Shakespeare' innumerable under his name *says* Mdeilmm he is not writing, he is speaking. Afterward one has to manage to write. I stagger.

—Those speaking tables, says my son, are *always* hoaxes. I'm telling you.

—Are you sure? I say.

—Yes, says my son, without hesitation.

—That doesn't mean one can't find a certain number of advantages in them.

I say that after a silence-of-meditation during which I made one of those psychic excursions

—comparable to hallucinations with one difference: if one plunges accidentally by daydream to land without transition in a yesteryear, going thus from August 2021 to year 49, year 1 in the transfiguration of my father into a disappeared reappeared in Presence in the world of other Presences, it is in full consciousness and without effort that one returns to the ground floor of time—

—a little trip to the land of spirits. On this occasion the spirits were not visible, and if I call upon the services of this vague word, 'spirit', it's because I don't have a practical term to designate that sensation or illusion of voice(s) that whispers or that whisper to me suddenly a whole luminous flowering of words. Come from somewhere, these words act suddenly like passkeys, they are the Words, the light-formulas. I imagine the sensation of a beacon in Baudelaire's head, a lance of fire, the impression of having one's eyes filled with thorns when Moses describes the violent effect of his migraine, the joy in the terror, the teeth of God that bite your tongue

—One cannot say that all these brain storms that apocalypse us are not real. The impression of powerlessness that such a brief instant of superpower causes is explained by the excessiveness of the objects put into communication: it's a matter of the marriage of the infinitely great with the infinitely small.

In a crisis of illumination, Baudelaire felt that his head was occupied by an indescribably gigantic machine, a telescope searching for a verbal star whose weak rays were explained by its distance at the very end of the times of times.

It occurs to me that Mdeilmm is the capsule into which many thousands of particles of Shakespeare's language have been thrown

I feel I am in the state of researcher who is tracking the trace of the birth of the universe. Unfortunately, my soul's eye is desperately weak

And Baudelaire didn't find,

And, in the end, Baudelaire didn't find, he was all of a sudden found, struck, knocked over, upset, pierced through by a fiery arrow

So I spell it out: M,d,e,i,l—

And now, Fanfares, trumpets, salvos. What is that? It's the sisterless hour in the night of Revelation, it's Act II of the tragedy of *Hamlet*, whose Scene IV must not be communicated to anyone,

Everything is said, and everything that is said is silenced and buried under the ground of forgetting where God the mole gravedigs.

Old Mole! It's you! Old mole and revered Papa!

I want to cry out: I found it! I pick up the telephone. And there, it's cut off

I woke up in the amazement of the Revenants to Self. One receives the Message, the Notice of Revelation only to return it to black matter.

Fortunately, a cry escaped, for I had no memory. According to my son, I let out a Molement. According to my daughter, I said that Georges, my father, was the champion of races under the text. I told my doctor that my mouth was full of earth. It's a rather rare symptom in the Syndrome of Alice in Wonderland.

—I don't have a lot of experience in the matter of ghosts, says my daughter. My daughter is eating cereal. This cereal is her cereal, I see clearly that she is not worried, either by the swarm of flakes or by the word 'cereal'. She eats regularly. It's reality without feverishness. Do only words come back as ghosts?

When I was simultaneously differently in two realities, the other day, which was a day other, I didn't return, I didn't get over it, one of the two was sequestered, it's perpetuity that is hell. It would be one thing if I had dreamed up myself, but everything was in the buildings of reality

—Recount it to me, says my friend the doctor. According to her, we were probably in a sort of forest for children. As a little girl less than ten years old we were several scattered like motionless flowers, seen from the back in a partial clearing, the walk had come to a standstill. If it were a matter of the Alice in Wonderland syndrome, she expected that I would see somewhere in the vision an excessive mushroom loom up like a house. Or a tree. I don't see the mushroom. However, the idea of seeing myself from behind awakens an acute curiosity. The reality on the left was (is) veiled by that fog secreted by myopia.

I recounted:

But where I expected my story to my surprise the chapter *Communications* presents itself.

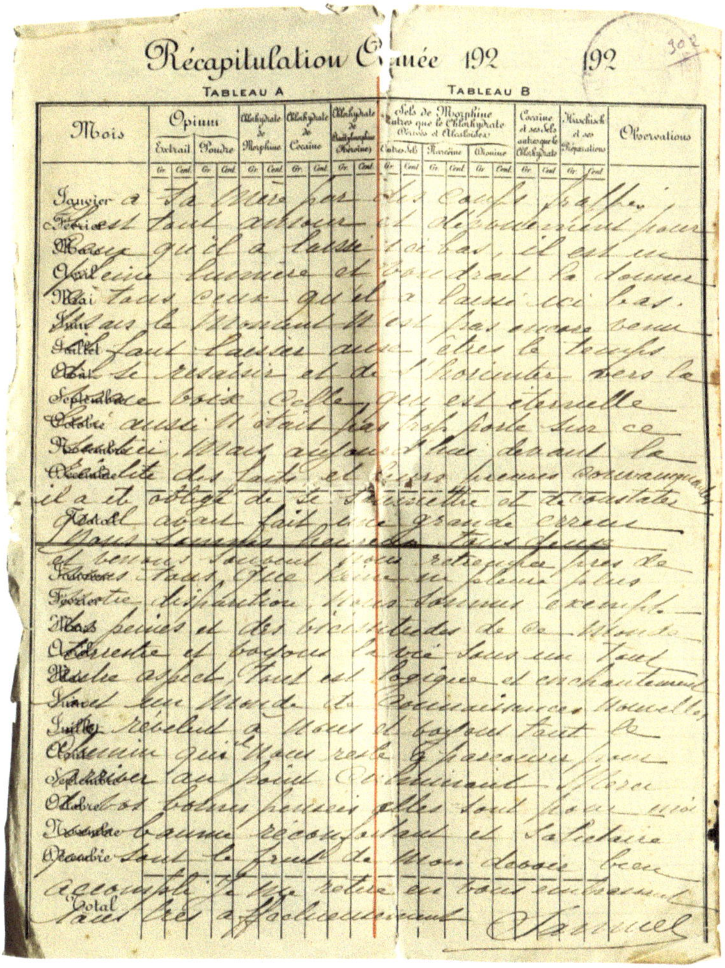
Récapitulation Année 192 192
Tableau A
Tableau B
Mois
Opium
Extrait
Poudre
Chlorhydrate de Morphine
Chlorhydrate de Cocaïne
Chlorhydrate de Diacétylmorphine (Héroïne)
Sels de Morphine autres que le Chlorhydrate Dérivés et Alcaloïdes
Autres Sels
Narcéine
Dionine
Cocaïne et ses Sels autres que le Chlorhydrate
Haschisch et ses Préparations
Observations
Gr.
Cent.
Janvier
Février
Mars
Avril
Mai
Juin
Juillet
Août
Septembre
Octobre
Novembre
Décembre
Total

enfants et leur porter mon affection
Mais surtout pas de larmes
ni de peine cela me fait souffrir
et ternir mon bonheur .. La lutte
a été grande pour moi et maintenant
c'est le calme et paisible repos
laissez-moi dans ce charme de cette
vie nouvelle, c'est le réconfort c'est
la consolation et l'épanouissement
de moi même Que, ceux qui
croient cherche la verité, elle est
éternelle, elle renferme dans son sein
tout ce que Dieu a créé et que
j'admire je suis un grand
chercheur cela développe mes facultés
c'est un travail intelligent et instructif
que ce fait en moi et qui me
donne la clef du grand Mystere
que beaucoup ignorent. Enfin je
termine mes pensées dans ce domaine
pour vous dire que je serais toujours
votre fidele protecteur, car je vous
aime tous bien et vous embrasse
de toute l'ardeur de mon âme
Georges

IV

THE COMMUNICATIONS

Communications

Today a day of resurrection there took place the totally unforeseeable Event: I find on the round table a thick bundle of slightly yellowed pages, remarkable for a regular craftsmanship: the paper filled with a writing of an almost military regularity, which allows for no interval, no fantasy, or paragraph break, the lines follow one another rhythmically at the pace of a muscular calligraphy, of a large size, these continual sentences seem to have been written while holding one's breath for a time that defies the capacity of a human breath. Alone, detached, solemn, like a severed head, just before the paper runs out one can make out a signature that is there to reassure and welcome the deep-diving reading out of breath, as if to signify: 'I am here, *ici, hier*, and today'. They are Letters, all by the same hand,   visibly that of an exceptionally large person, almost motionless, it moves so slowly, majestic or monumental. One might think that a Roman statue is the author of these lines. The signatories, 'Georges', 'Samuel', men, affirmed, one sees that they don't suspect a thing. They were fathers. From father to father, sometimes the signatory has the sceptre sometimes they are a pair, a co-signature that has sway, and I notice in outline the effigies of Toth and Râ, father grand-father son brother of writing. Within this vision, Râ is bearded and imposing like Samuel the father of my father, the founder, the other, the young man with the shining eyes and the long gaze, who looks very much like the sacred ibis, is indeed Georges Toth the double of my father, the inventor of remedies for the deterioration of memory

But while the scribe's hand is always unalterably the same over several decades beginning in the 30s, the nature of the supports is miscellaneous: it's no-matter-what, lined pages, prescription pages for pharmaceutical preparations, unattached pages, all in different colours, a notable trait that contrasts these unmatched signs with the mechanical regularity of the graphic design. One might think that the writing hand has been surprised during sleep thus in a state of unpreparation, as if the message were already underway, and one had to jump on the paper as onto a tram or a train, a dream, while one is not dressed there is only a used envelope on the round table. The broadcast has already begun

This hasty pile

It is *the legacy of Alice.* The Stolen Legacy. The traveller without address. The neglected, the abandoned, the misrecognized, destiny asleep under the centuries that wakes up to the ecstasy of the archaeologist who never dared to hope for it,

Arrived, naked, enigmatic jumble, seeks reading,

Saved! preserved in some trunk delivered over to the tribulations of History and —to my dazzled stupefaction —I say to my daughter —a treasure of an incalculable value opens up, sparkling, before my eyes, and has no other equivalent but what dazzled the eyes of William Legrand, during the truly incredible discovery he made, on Sullivan Island, of the most fantastic of real treasures, as reported by a direct witness of this revelation, the poet Edgar Allan Poe. One remembers a communication that the famous dead man made to our Alice —and as I was about to ask in what language Poe addressed Alice, it was specified that it was in Baudelaire's language that Mr Poe had wanted to transmit his brotherly feelings to Alice Carisio, medium-writer. There is nothing surprising about that, for among theosophists, spiritualists, poets and dreamers, there are always many languages ready to transmit Communications. The spiritual proximity of certain members of my family with Baudelaire, as with Hugo, is well known.

(If I had time I could recall here a fact worthy of learned reveries, or psychoanalytic deductions, concerning my mother and Baudelaire, and the Shakespearian scene where, posthumously, they assert their opposition to which I am witness and naturally on the side of my mother, but I will perhaps do that in another chapter, or perhaps not)

Here there would have been a chapter titled *Alice and Mr. Pot or Peau*. Or Po: this Gentleman allegedly presented himself as an envoy from Those Above. He is supposed to have revealed the winning number of the next drawing of the national Lottery. Thanks to her extranatural memory, Alice claimed to have noted down the twenty-four numbers on the back of a prescription form. She had in truth found a ticket bearing this number at the ticket seller's in the Place d'Armes. All of 54 is witness to the moments of the affair. In the end, the drawing. 54 is divided. Mr Pot's number comes out. Widespread emotion. Alice sends Mr Emile. The ticket is reimbursable. Alice's honour is safe and with it that of the Theosophy of Oran

But Eve my mother, when she relays this news, recommends that I 'drop it'. She herself does not remember the order of her successive feelings during 'the ticket affair', which had a discreet echo on the four floors of 54. Except for the reaction of Omi my German grandmother, second floor. 'Jetzt muss ich lachen,' she says. But the other floors don't understand German.

Like William Legrand and Edgar Allan Poe panting for breath, I too will not try to describe the feelings with which I contemplated this paper treasure, these flashes and splendours of visions that sprung from this confused heap of soiled old papers saturated with sentences where I saw the gold and gems of imagination.

My amazed and lasting exaltation has that quality of naive joy that I felt when I was five, an auspicious time for fertile indecisions and the jubilatory adherence to fantastic theories—on the condition that they are adorned with shiny fake jewels, balls of multicoloured glass, pearls, veils, and populated by magical presences, feminine beauties, apparitions of maternal queens

I have always madly loved fake stars, that is, true stars of the imagination, the unlimited riches of magical poems, the glistening lights of the ribbons sold by the metre in the novelty shop of my grandfather Prospero Samuel Cixous, master of the *Deux Mondes*, at the corner of the street of the Military Circle. At age five I had a beau, Ariel Flörsheim, a child of German refugees, able to do all sorts of real and imaginary acrobatics, who almost ended up as a parachutist in the American army, which will surprise no one for Ariel was born for the air, and afterwards is one of the spirits waiting for his story, which I promise myself I will do in any case before my death, for after I don't think I will write, according to Alice 'one never knows', according to my mother the idea that I will be able to write after my death is one of those *Quatsch!* that continue to infiltrate into my memory from the ceiling of the fourth floor, 54 rue Philippe in Oran. For me the real jewels are the false ones, those without commercial value that have an inestimable value, and for which I am capable of all sorts of excesses, I can steal, I withdraw rapturously to the island where eternally I rejoin the family of refugees from Milan and all those inhabitants who change their looks and their genders in rapid and impressive changes like actors, where one moves at the speed of a dream through free metamorphoses.

Seen up close, the Pile is a thick assortment of Notices of weddings and deaths, headless newspaper clippings, Letters, bills for orders of hats caps and berets a certificate of French naturalization with the seal of the Emperor, traces of footsteps or allusions to a crowd of unknowns with common and mysterious biblical names, and strangely repeated in a same list of characters set up in columns, probably in order of urgency importance or entry into the memory of Reine the queen our grandmother, in power on the third floor, and by metonymy on the second and fourth floors.

Enter, right here p. 117, the Queen Reine—Reine is her name and her function. Mémé is a nickname used only between the second and third floors. Mémé's geopolitical situation is illustrated by her position between the second, the floor of the *Aufklärung*, the Enlightenment and the Categorical Imperative-to-the-extent-possible, a Kantian morality not dog-eared but modernized given the powerful changes for the worse to the world's soul, in this time of plagues and burning darkness. The second floor believes in life, its unfortunate fragilities and its finitude, nothing but life. Denizens of the second floor do not frequent cemeteries, don't monologue with tombs, what is more there are none in their mental space

and the fourth floor, region of Visitations, hotel of guardian angels and postfuturist Main Post Office, station of the dead happy to have enjoyment of Peace and spiritual aides,

Meanwhile Reine, our sovereign grandmother, goes her third-floor way balanced between the wars, between the floor without angels, armed with books and foreign languages, and the ahistorical floor with angels, embassy for the Supreme Spirit spread everywhere a little in all the rooms like a scent of dried roses. Reine says nothing and thinks in silence. Reine is the feminine of *Rien*, nothing. It sometimes happens that she receives Letters transmitted by Alice and signed Samuel, her husband, or Georges, her son, in Alice's hand. Alice's hand is careful and manicured as it ought to be to carry out such a virtuosic and delicate mission as that of the assistant of the Communicants. As a High Official in the Two-Worlds, Alice, despite her modest income as a pharmacy assistant, is always dressed up. Mémé's hands are strong like those of a man skilled at all kinds of work. No finery. The sovereign wears the house-keeper's apron of the third floor.

I don't know what Mémé—Reine of the third floor—thinks of the habit that her husband Samuel seems to have, once deceased, of frequenting the fourth. And consequently of confiding to Alice, the mailperson, his thoughts and his advice addressed to his widow, Reine.

I know what Eve my mother thinks of this mediation, she does not hide it. Once, one unique time, my mother became aware of a letter signed Georges, it was shortly after his death, but I will come back to that later

NB. Here, note what The Cousin says:

—Domination of Mémé, through the exertion of a force of soul that was almost animal for never expressed verbally, but expressed by a silence of majesty, and especially an aristocratic slowness. Mémé's motto: 'Why do it faster (for example peel carrots or other vegetables) *when one has the time*?

Thus they were not as dead as people thought, these high dead of the family, these kings, these judges, these great travellers in unknown lands, these precursors in the two lives, on one side and the other of the demise, there under my eyes, they were like those gods at the mythological microphone, fully active as spiritual advisers, I say to myself while glancing, with rapid heartbeat, at these miraculous messages

Reine always knew to keep silent, does not complain, with one exception: Howls of a wounded animal on the grave of her beloved son (my father) let loose within the confines of the place of mourning and cut off sharply at the exit from the place of weeping. This absolute mastery is exerted also when she finds herself brutally exposed to attempts at destabilization, acts of indiscretion, unwarranted familiarity inconvenient interventions by those close to her, neighbours, cousins. When Alice lets her know that 'Samuel has come', she seems to remark sovereignly the level of familiarity emanating from the messenger's voice. She uses the formal address with Alice, likewise with Eve my mother, the wife of the 'Son'. That she adores the Son, the Unique, is absolutely nobody's business. Samuel and Georges use the familiar address with Alice. Victor Hugo does the same with Shakespeare. No one knows if Shakespeare does this spontaneously or if he ends up giving in to the muscular force of Hugo's familiar address, for its only after hours of discussion between the two men, at 1.30 in the morning Wednesday 25 January 1854, the meeting having begun at 9.30 in the evening, that the English genius and his interpreter the round table, which resists hard-headedly with its four feet, becomes agitated, contorts, gives in to the naive and stubborn pressure of the great Frenchman, unless the couple give in from fatigue, and at the end of their defensive terseness. For hours—as the record of these matches between titans make clear—Shakespeare courteously dodges the urgent necessity to Hugolize himself, his responses (for he *responds*, he doesn't start the duel) are craftily calculated to safeguard indeterminacy. Far from the long harangues that his English-speaking characters, all those clans of the tormented, unfurl without detour in front of everyone, Shakespeare, for his part, battles with great economy, coolly avoiding the countless traps of French, managing to maintain amiable ambiguities, in short without calling attention to it able to maintain the ruse of the indecision of his native *You* despite his situation as a fellow exile on an island where the Frenchman can proclaim himself to be the last Frenchmen and the first European on an equal footing with his fellow genius, the French language being neither hegemonic or colonialist but simply natural and hospitable to the brother geniuses, he, Hugo, proclaims.

NB. According to Mr Emile, there is a relation at the very least telepathic and perhaps very supernaturally real between Victor Hugo and Alice's gift. Mrs Carisio tyrant mother of twelve children supposedly attended one of the enormous public demonstrations in homage to Victor Hugo, in 1881 or 1885, being pregnant and perhaps with Alice. According to Mr Emile, that would explain—the ways of the God of any religion being comparable to the circulation of global news in the twenty-first century—the monumental presence of the twenty volumes of the works of the master, the only earthly God for Samuel, in the storeroom with shelves on the third floor. That spicy exotic and familiar scent in the third-floor apartment was the presence of Hugo and his emanations.

To come back to the declaration of The Cousin—The family of Samuel (father of my father, Oran's double of Victor Hugo by the dignified and assured aspect of his authority): poor. Mémé has no money. She sends clothes in all directions. Samuel has two brothers, Moses and Abraham, each has twelve children, twenty-four paupers, among whom several named Moses and several Abraham. Samuel speaks of his son Georges as 'the socialist'. Other times, wanting to strike the family's imagination, he says 'the doctor'. An occasion is cited when the father designates the son his pride, the one he loves, as 'the Idiot'. The father gets the Idiot out of trouble when he is caught up in the snares of a totally impossible affair of passion. The father dies carried off by an attack right after the resolution. He becomes almost immediately a very active spirit. Alice is no longer idle. Satisfaction. Ideal of the paternal ego. Self-affirmation that the whole family reinforces by a veritable personality cult. Except for Reine who says not a word. Leaves all the words to Alice.

She calls Georges 'my Son', he's her son and her pride. I don't remember having heard my grandmother invite 'Samuel' or 'my husband' into her sober speech.

With time the twenty-four offspring all married with boy cousins girl cousins interabrahamized and selfmosesified become more and more numerous with littler and littler ones, there are more and more abrahamosesified children. The Cousin takes the direction between the Claires and the Deborahs, I get lost. The little people of mice, a tribe with a lot of heart, is unified towards the direction of the Queen Reine—Because no one has a telephone, cousins arrive on the third floor without warning, after an earthquake or a wound. Among the remarkable features of these movements: the family does not tear itself apart. An instinct—for lack of a telephone—guides the family members, which lets them avoid traffic jams. Alice seems to have played the role of news central.

On this subject, The Cousin underscores the capital role of the black Telephone—so black that an aura of starless night emanates from it, an impressive and Taboo Telephone. It would not occur to anyone to use it or even to touch it unless it's with a brief glance slid beneath heavily fringed eyelids.

The Telephone is the sceptre the crown the dog, the sacred sword, the aeroplane, the archangel of the God of the Abrahams, Isaacs, Jacobs. It follows and precedes my father the doctor-saint everywhere, any human and even animal individual, belonging to the intrafamilial and friendly cousinhood who might be in danger, who might be suffering or anxious can call it at any hour of day or night

If the Rescuer goes from the second floor to the third floor where he might go to provide care and counsel to Deborah The Invalid born-to-be-cared-for or to eat the Couscous set aside for the Son by the mother and only for Him, the Telephone goes up with him calm, solid, admirable in its constancy like the dog of a blind man. Of all the blind men who turn towards the Light-Itself.

—'If anyone called him, he went,' reports The Cousin. I don't remember the Telephone animated by the soul of a dog, but The Cousin will never forget it. I remember the Dog-son-of Georges who died from the death of his father. He followed Georges everywhere going beyond himself. And if Alice had received Visits in Algiers and not only in Oran, she would no doubt have passed on Communications from this Spirit mad with love and rage.

Visits: each time that visits came unannounced for lack of a telephonic medium (Alice functioning only for the people of the Beyond, it's her speciality as medium-writer, agent for the two continents of the Initiated) Mémé, giving up her bed of majesty, following the Law of third-floor Hospitality, occupies as a consequence the bed of The Cousin, who then slept with Aunt Deborah, Aunt Deborah sleeping on the quiet with the

dead, if one can call sleeping these chaste and passionate relations with those handsome men that the briefness of their passage on earth sanctifies with an erotic glory. Deborah adores the
white trousers of her heroes. Legend of the white trousers: how
the idols slipped the stirring trousers, discreet banners of their
virility, under the double mattresses, so that the night would iron
them and give them back their stylishness.

—I sense that Blaise Pascal died at age thirty-nine like my
father. This presentiment is followed by a meditation on the
occult relations among those Inspired in opposite ways: one
cannot imagine more, less, Christian, Jewish, believer, lover of
Man, hero of Charity, gratuitous, secular, mystical, socialist,
committed, not at all, devoted without condition, with condi-
tions, than these two young men. The same brilliant gaze, large
nose of a bird ready to fly. But my father does not weep. These
Communications flout what we call reality or illusion, impossible possible, they are indifferent to all this timidity, they turn
and they cause to turn, they are able, they come to those who
want on behalf of the Other, the dead one saved from the lions
and pythons.

—With these Communications, says my daughter, it's not
surprising that you became haunted without knowing it

—I was not informed, I say, I didn't know that the spirits
frequented the fourth floor. I was a little citizen of the second
floor. It's the house that was haunted, the gold of paper and
whisperings had currency only over our heads. But there was
Alice-for-children. There was Alice-and-Mr Emile. And the
Emergency Pharmacy, called Plato's Pharmacy of Oran, where

the preparers of solutions, balms, remedies, powders, pills, pearls, necklaces and potions officiated, he at night and she during the day.

There is relation between Alice Carisio of Oran and Alice in wonderland, according to the neurological psychiatrists, an emanation from the migraines of her adoptive bard Charles Dodgson in reality. The form of Our Alice was in fact like a macro-optical enlargement of a seven-year-old girl, six times oversized by Todd's Syndrome. Let's look at this group photo in the box of caps coming from France for the Hat Shop of the Deux Mondes. One sees only Her: a giant, whose presence lying on the chaise longue before a row of normal-sized people fills the frame in such proportions that the over-burdened photo leaned to the right, ready to tip over like an ill-balanced boat. An impression of partial palinopsia shakes me, I stumble, I lean on my Cousin, and recover by training my gaze on the head and body of Mr Emile, whose size and look, somewhat similar to my father's appearance reassured me. It is not I, it is Alice who is odd, and so strongly so that when I shift my gaze from her macro-volume to the space around her person, as a result the room is necessarily immense, at least for a few moments.

Seen from the teeming and quivering little street,

It's up there, on the fourth and last floor, that all of the supernatural personnel live: the magicians, the dead, the officials of the marvellous, all the powers mixed up with distressing fra-gilities, over which watch Alice-and-Mr-Emile, perpetually on duty, and both of them, sister and brother assistants at the

Emergency Pharmacy, the palace of care and assistance located on the Other Side of the Place d'Armes. 54 rue Philippe, fourth floor, a balcony with a view of the sacred places in the distance, it's logical since spirits at that time were lodged up above and not down below as happened in the time of Ulysses and Circe.

Seen from above by the spirits, the so-called fourth floor is the first floor, the landing strip for the floating spirits when they come on a humanitarian mission and present themselves at the border crossing between those from above and those from below, where awaits them Alice the Appointed One, the most secretive character and thus the most extraordinary, indecipherable being of the little people of 54. A Presence whose status is unique, which naturally explains that she has always been designated by a single name like the head of state, she is Alice, the way Tiresias the polysexual or like Joan or any other corporeal emanation spokesperson for those Above, ancestors of the young ladies of the telephone, all those persons with a variable sexual definition, endowed with a hearing sensitive enough to hear the voices inaudible to the average human

Alice was no doubt an ultimate revival of those demi-deities that one still saw in the streets of imperial Rome, seated beneath the arcades and exercising the function of public scribe for women, which would explain her colossal stature and her divine impassiveness. Mr Emile told me a secret in the right ear, the ear of secrets people say: Alice, in one of the ancient centuries, was supposedly a student of Augustine, a teacher at Annaba. It's there that she would have learnt the art of Correspondence, her diplomacies, her active and crafty *sancta prudentia*, her stubborn patience.

When I want to relate Alice's mysteries, a dizziness over-
takes me, the lines on the page go wild, an assault, entangle-
ments followed by crossed-out crossings out, it's the alert, I am
in total collapse, I am terribly cold, I am burning up, then it is
daylight in the middle of the night and the real nightmare with-
draws like an abrupt tide.

The cause of the crisis is the double nature of the subject
and of me. It's because before me there are two simultaneous
Lives of Alice-and-Mr-Emile, the Carisios. As the one charged
with a narration, how to be faithful when I need to be two
witnesses at the same time? It is very difficult. There exist in fact
two types of Carisian manifestations. Like two fantastic spec-
tacles, the one takes place in a golden world where the spirits
for children circulate. In the other world, that of the spirits for
adults, everything is mourning, paleness, and life is at the price
of death.

Now I was only ever an eyewitness, in person, of the golden
world and the barley-sugar treats. What I know about the other
world, the one whose archives I have just received, I am aware
of only through what my mother confided. Until last week, no
one suspected the existence of this treasure of traces.

I might never have known anything of this other world that
was playing out above our heads and in our brains during the
whole time that Carisian Civilization prospered from top to
bottom of 54.

At the heart of the treasure, after a methodical search, one
will find *the prayer*. One might never have discovered it. Still
feeling the surprise, I confide the event to my son: the existence

of a spiritual object of an inestimable value. It is my father himself par excellence, that is to say, His Spirit, that made a gift of these all-powerful Words, 'sacred and precious words in the events of earthly life,' I quote here the words of 'my Father all powerful Spirit of Georges' taken down under His Dictation by Alice at work. The Dictating One is explicit: 'This prayer of a great power and efficacity can and can be worn only by persons worthy to wear it on themselves.' Preferably in the lining of a jacket.

Le 7 Mai 1965

Ma chère Sœur,

Je viens vers toi pour te dire que je suis heureux de pouvoir t'assister dans les luttes constantes que tu traverses tant physiques que morales. Sache surtout que notre présence est souvent près de vous tous et qu'aucune distinction ne vous sépare où vous sommes, nous voyons tout objectivement sans y ajouter aucune importance particulière. Maintenant parlons un peu de ta santé qui est très précaire, je vais faire de mon mieux pour te donner satisfaction. Je te vois bien anéantie, cela coule de source on a le devoir à nous, et veux me rendre utile et agréable pour te faire plaisir. Tout d'abord je te dirai que ton organisme ressent des troubles dûs au changement de climat qui est tout autre que celui d'Algérie, que ton état déficient t'occasionne des difficultés pour être en forme pour assurer ton travail ce qui est un handicap pour toi. Donc pour ces douleurs qui viennent se greffer dans ton organisme. Je conseille votre chère Alice de bien vouloir consulter le formulaire pharmaceutique qui était notre guide pour bien des cas, et de te remettre la formule du Baume antirhumatismal

qui y est inscrit, afin que tu puisses en faire
l'usage, à moins que tu fasses de la médecine
homéopatique ce qui n'est pas recommandé donc
ne l'emploie pas. Maintenant ma chère sœur une
autre question me vient à l'esprit, c'est que je tiendrai
à ce que tu portes sur toi une prière d'une grande
puissance et efficacité, celle que porte sur elle
la famille Caruso, il faut être digne pour
l'avoir sur soi et toi tu es dans le cas. Ces noms
sont sacrés et précieux dans les événements de la vie
terrestre.
J'attends qu'Élie les mentionne car elle les
fait par cœur. Prière

Barrasasa — Letitia Recella, Agla, Agla, Tétragrammaton
Adonay, Grand Dieu tout Puissant. Secourez-moi
tout indigne que je sois. Délivrez-moi de tout danger
de la mort de l'âme et de celle du corps et de
embûches de mes ennemis, tant visibles qu'invisibles.
Dieu, Ely, Eloï, Ela, Sabbaoth, Adonay, que tous
ces saints noms me soient profitables et salutaires
à moi qui suis la servante de Dieu.

Voici ma chère sœur toutes mes
recommandations. Je vous embrasse tous
très respectueusement

—Do you have this prayer? cries my confidante. Why haven't you transmitted it? But I want to know where you got this! It's unbelievable! I knew nothing about this!

—I received it too late, I say. I try to present my case. This prayer was transmitted to Deborah, that is, transmitted by 'the spirit Georges' to Alice with the mission of transmitting it to the Worthy Ones, beginning with His Fervent Deborah the Invalid-Born-to-be-Cared-for. At Alice's address, the prayer of His Superior Spirit-my-dead-father was transmitted by means of her medium. I don't know anything.

—By telephone? Telepathy? Did my father His Superior Spirit wake Alice during the night? At what time? Precisely? Unforeseeable? Or in the middle of the street? At table? In what circumstances, states of the medium, state of the sky, warnings? auguries? none? With what frequency? Regularly?

You see that the Communications last as long or as far as the paper support allows. Once the pages are saturated, it's finished on the support. Nothing proves that the Communication did not continue in another way. Or else the interruption might have been caused by Alice's exhaustion. Nothing is known about the endurance of the real physical body of the missionary. I would like to know what affects opened up or were unleashed or not in Alice's very vast envelope. How did it end? Fainting? Transport? In certain cases, the medium is raised as much as 30 centimetres from the ceiling in a prone position, that's where she is comfortably installed, as she can see with her own eyes for she sees herself both from below and from above. This position is called the Alice Syndrome in the Mirror. During this trance, the beneficiary feels a lightness that is described as like that of an angel: an immense, material and imponderable body. The duration of this experience is not fixed. However, the Letter that resulted from all these phenomena looks ordinary.

When I was in bireality, the state lasted from 3.15 in the afternoon until 7 that evening and afterward I had no message to transmit.

It's enough to become aware of the Communications to sense that the medium, if she feels perhaps some malaise of strangeness, is filled with that bliss that intoxicates to tears the great ecstatics. These Letters, all of them without exception, and through the years, emit a same level of happiness, that sort of sensation of sublime satisfaction that you taste after having made love and that lasts an hour without limit without urgency without burning of desire. The mystics call this state the after-fire. It's a subtle essence that combines nothingness and birth. This spiritual perfume is more perceptible still upon reading the letters of Samuel. The Communication provokes in Alice's whole large body the man's odour that floated around Samuel when he posed for photographic eternity in the Zouave costume. His beard was black and shining. The beard said: 'You see how I am thinking of you, my pet?' The Handsome Zouave is an advertisement for Mr Emile, maker of Colognes for soldiers and photographic medium. Mr Emile is always clean-shaven, on Sunday, Alice's day, Samuel frequents the Moorish Baths at the end of rue Philippe. The Spirit maintains the signals of its body.

Deborah-ill-health who was always listening to the incessant chattering of her ovaries of a premature baby abdominably feels the secret attractions that impregnate the Communications.

If I could recount the Secret Life of Deborah the Virgin, which my aunt confided to me while taking me to her favourite temple the Pharmacy, you would see her reel from one deborizing passion to another, her innocence and her spiritual purity fluttering around the father around the brother, brushing the licking flames with her feeble well-ironed wings, content with their early deaths that kept them in the brilliance of their impressive beauty, one heart for two just for her. Between the man of fifty and the man of thirty, I think she leaned towards the son. Maybe not: confiding in me daughter of the son was she not drawn by my carnal presence? Skinny Deborah quivers under the blow from the sacred paper.

The Prayer

—'My dear Sister

I come to you to tell you that I am happy

—Then I am too, I was sure that you would come,

—Don't interrupt me, Deborah, concentrate —I was saying
—I'm waiting for Alice to reconnect—

am happy to be able to help you in the constant struggles
you are traversing —with an s, Alice —both physical and moral.
Know above all that our Presence is often near you and that no
distinction separates us where we are we see everything objec-
tively without giving it any particular importance . . .'

Here Deborah blows her very large nose with a large hand-
kerchief of the dear saintly brother who always had a cold like
her. Blowing her nose makes a growling sound. What shakes up
the addressee is the date: today 8 May, Georges's birthday

—Are you going to blow your nose for a long time?

Who says that? Georges or Samuel? The distinction separates no one thinks Deborah.

The Prayer is Found the Day of His Birthday, this thought
traverses Deborah's body like lightning.

—If it doesn't bother you I would really like to sit down, excellent brother for my back hurts

— . . . I would say that your organism . . . your state of deficiency . . . which is a handicap for you . . . these pains that graft themselves onto your organism . . . our dear Alice . . .

and on these words skinny Deborah in rapture feels her soul take on weight by transfer from Alice's overabundance

Large excessively vast slow like the *Alice*, an ocean liner that has just raised anchor, still much slower than Mémé, floating, the waking sleep of a whale who delicately rocks the Jonas of her entrails, Alice is in a state of bliss with eyes half-closed. An exceptional woman and something other than a woman, not only something of a whaling boat tossing from side to side and in the trance of voluptuousness something of the whale, but also a landscape of Oran, hills, on her promontory is spread out as on a jeweller's counter a row of fat pearls grazing lazily like half-sleeping cows. On the summit bouquets of tiny curls of silver hair. Those motionless blue eyes, copies of the motionless eyes of Mme Blavatsky, which easily fascinated the generation of poets contemporary with Alice, Mr Emile, Yeats, Joyce, Kafka, Einstein

The nights when Alice doesn't sleep, there is a queue, for some reason or another the dead are in a hurry, there is going to be war, a birthday, the great house-moving, change of address or continent, it changes nothing for 'Us' but if *You* forget us, it is in vain that we are dead with the newly dead from the second floor and the third, Alice's army fills out. They are more and more numerous on the Other Side. Alice's worry: her succession. Who can replace her if she leaves her post vacant? She can't count on the candidates who are all weak in body or mind. The Worry prevents her from leaving. However at the thought that on the Other Side she would have to change her activity, once she has retired as the medium-translator on duty, and from then on draw from the depths of her sole Spirit the wisdom of an indisputable philosophical and dietetic efficacity, and for that have only the instrument of her bare soul, because in Passing she will have had to shed her colossal envelope, it's complete collapse. It's because she doesn't know what the soul looks like when it is liberated from its dead body. Obscurely she lets herself count on Georges's help, but there's no guarantee.

—Microbe!

—Who is calling her? My father. Microbe! My father's voice is lively and transparent like the water in the fountain at the end of rue Philippe. First seated is Alice who fills a fifth of the dining room, at the corner of the Friday table, then the table is pushed into the space left free and the twelve guests take their places. She absorbs her dishes following Dr Steiner's instructions. Dr Steiner advises her by thought during the meal.

—Microbe! My father forms a large fish's mouth with his two hands. Hypnotized Alice yawns widely, you can see her broad pink tongue, my father closes his hands. Alice closes her jaw. Mémé mashes her carrots with eyes lowered.

Dr Steiner eats hard-boiled eggs. He was very close to Christ, Kafka notes. Not Alice. She has fun with Jesus. Not

Christ. He too is part of the freemasonry interested in lower breaths as in higher breaths. Alice is interested in intestinal winds. Like Shakespeare, she considers that the Low was created in the image of the High.

Alice does not go to mass. Those from above were coming. Where? —It went on in the dining room, I believe, says The Cousin. Or elsewhere. It was very intimate.

Once, for her tenth birthday, my Cousin received a Communication from Samuel: —'My Darling, you farted in front of Jesus, your asshole is going to be sewed up.' The queen of the third floor doesn't really believe it. Her husband would never use any of those salacious verbal units. Wisely, the third floor tolerates that Alice is a medium-writer and doesn't think less of her

—I am meditating, says Alice. —That doesn't surprise me, says the young Eve my mother.

Hidden meanings are cultivated.

There are those who hear. Alice doesn't hear the voices. She doesn't see them. She is *called*. There are presences that cut off communication. All the people who are not convinced or who are astonished a little disturb the callers.

There are Manifestations. An object that falls: Samuel is annoyed. Blows struck. It's the black telephone. It's the evening. One has to be in *a certain state*. We have information about the state of Mr Emile, when there is a visitation: his eyes are half-closed, he is sitting straight up in his rocking chair and is talking to himself. On Alice's state, what is certain is that no one knows anything. From the extreme regularity of the handwriting, the large size of the letters, one may conclude that the (internal) dictation happens at a slow and constant rhythm. The Dead let their advice flow in an even stream and at medium speed. It is nothing like the stormy, feverish, hoarse output of the Spirit of Hamlet's Father, those strangled cries, those fits of nervous coughing, that sudden stuttering, those groans torn from the throat of a gasping ghost, that insistence. Style has also its time, the sentence follows the model of politeness that has currency at the very beginning of the twentieth century.

Often the Communications coincide: they arrive very close to the events. A week after my father's death. For Deborah, this is proof. Right away she goes to the Pharmacy so Alice can weigh her. She has not lost weight.

I return to the Prayer

Georges:

My dear sister, one must be worthy to have It on you, and you are worthy. Words are precious in earthly life.

I'm waiting for Alice to mention them for she knows them by heart . . .

I was saying to myself that by force of will and by bringing to bear all one's spiritual weight, and perhaps with the mental help of Dr Steiner who treats with colours—and the Carisio dining room is populated with objects in sacred colours—Alice would manage involuntarily to stir us if not the soul itself, at least the imagination. There was thus a prayer. We were in the exacerbated state of the team that even as it doubts methodically accompanies Legrand who carries the scarab attached to a piece of string that he turns around himself, each moment carried away by a powerful curiosity, the next moment weighed down by boredom and scepticism. I was saying to myself that a century after the Communication, the prayer if there was one—faded yellowed, unreadable, outdated—would have lost its former powers like Mr Emile's herbs.

And the first word was: Barnasa.

At the fourth word, hilarity suddenly shakes my daughter's body, like a crisis of mystical tremblings.

A temple crumbles in the Orient of her thought. I will not put into words what my son thinks. It has a khaki colour. He didn't expect That.

—Because of the combination of signifiers belonging to different registers from pseudo-Hebrew to baby talk, one can't decide if the Prayer is a magical or comical formula says my daughter. She didn't expect That.

—Under the austere protection of my father the signatory delegating to Alice, everything leads one to think that the formula is serious

—My aunt Deborah, a worthy case, left instructions to her nephew Saul-co-theosopher that he make sure the Prayer was buried with her, so that, dead, she be guarded from invisible-enemies.

It is unknown whether Saul followed Alice's order

And the Prayer?

—People are going to believe, thinks the editor, that everything that precedes is but ashes simulation, the sooty remains of one of H's hallucinations. I see he thinks: yet another blow of Mdeilmm. —*Foutaise*, thinks my mother. It's the word that Georges taught her.

—In German, it is called *Krimskrams.*

And beneath its appearance of bullshit, the Prayer sows on the lower floors the seeds of ill-feeling. It's Zebrew, laughs Mr. Emile. Alice motionless.

Lanky Deborah lying down her gaze turned towards the photos of her men recites out loud: Barnasa . . .

Alice asks Ely Elou Ela to rescue her from the visible and invisible enemy whose name begins with E and ends with E, in her own name, for she is worried for the Spirits whom she serves with all her soul in imitation of Joan fighting out of love for the Dauphin and family. She joins her prayer to the complaints of her revered Georges and Samuel. The Father the Son and Alice conduct a trial against the intruder. The principal document without a doubt is Georges's—my father's—deposition for he is the husband of the aforementioned. One may admire the frankness, the steely soul, the choice of Justice, the courage in short of the declaration. An indictment. I will quote for example: 'I am often close to my dear children (G is talking about H and P) for they are very maleable (*sic*) and I inspire them so as to help them invisibly without their suspecting it for they need my spiritual support. My poor Eve is stuborn (*sic*) I cannot act with her she does not facilitate my fluidic current, which means that she does not receive my inspirations for she is profoundly resistant to the survival of the soul and that is a black mark. Her indifference to the celestial country interrupts me in my finest moments . . .'

I cut off there. Note: I have corrected only a small number of imperfections. I leave a few earthly signs, to serve as example.

What would the family do without the vigilant protection of Alice? What would Alice do without Georges's power, even partially cut off by E-E's obstinacy? What feelings are aroused in the mind of the addressees upon receiving these various militant storms? According to Samuel's (The Father's) expression: everyone is 'umbraged' on the third and fourth floors. The affective and spiritual waves caused by the presence of the foreign element E-E appear very sombre, a procession of worries, struggles, pains, sadnesses whereas Here it is calm and serene. He advises his beloved family to be patient and discreet.

—Eve is a mismatched piece in this world of the earthly and celestial 54. For those from Oran, how can one be a Germanjew, or, perhaps, a Jewishgerman, a chimera, I say to myself.

Alice wipes her lips with a large, immaculate damask napkin. The fabric is tinged with long blood-red traces.

—Was heisst 'Immaculate'? asks Omi my German grandmother, from the agnostic second floor. Mr. Emile makes an off-colour joke with the word immaculate and he laughs, he laughs.

In Alice's archives, various specialized publications: *Superior Worlds, Inferior Worlds, Farts and Peace,* * *The P of Einstein, Occult Music, Spiritualism for Children, What Jesus Ate, Learn to Write by Farting, How Poets Fart: Rimbaud, First Poems*

She doesn't laugh, laughter is for Mr Emile. Mr Emile talks nonsense. He's an artist. The lobe of his left ear is missing. A rat took it for a piece of cheese during his sleep. Alice had warned him. In vain. Since then, Mr Emile is a convert. Incredulity has a steep price. He believed so little in the Communication that he went to bed as soon as Alice began to write. My father also calls him Mr Emile. Mr Emile never goes out without his title. An old hat. I don't dare think that it was perhaps left unsold at Samuel's hat shop. At the beginning, the hat shop was called High Life (in English), that is, Iglif, a title whispered by the spirit of a 'count' of Alice's. I was initiated into cats by Mr Emile. On Sundays, we went to the 'Promenade de Létang' at dawn, there were more than a hundred of them. We carried the communion wafers, he had a bucket of libations full of sardine heads, heads without force, I had the newspapers on which to place the offerings at the base of the tall plane trees in Persephone's woods. There, at Mr Emile's call, while Ulysses whispers his

---

* In the original, this odd title is 'Pets et Paix'. The two words are homonyms in French and pronounced like the letter 'P' in the following title. [Trans.]

142

directives in his intact ear, I saw a crowd assemble running towards the trees with horrible meowings, a starving tribe, more shadows of cat than cats who, without Mr Emile's piety, would be a tribe of cadavers

There was a lady who asked his advice at the pharmacy for her husband who broadcast nauseating farts from the first balcony of the Opera. I was sitting on the magical skinny knees of Mr Emile. He prepared lozenges scented with violets for the lady. Since then, the gentleman's farts are violet-scented, the lady is happy at the Opera. I don't really believe this. I fall between his skinny knees from laughter. That's an exaggeration, I say. Mr Emile corrects me: exoneration. Mr Emile needs me in order to believe his story. I am important

—By dint of invoking the fourth-floor magicians, I saw the book I am now writing. On its cover it bore a name: *The True from False*. Black letters on a background of candy pink

The Cousin absolutely does not remember the candies. And yet, every year, and more precisely on every visit from Father Christmas, one could see that he had been there by the candies he placed at the foot of the tree, he or his animal and he.

Between the True and the False, how is one to make the distinction?

The rat, when he finds the bed full of Alice and Mr Emile, how does he choose his morsel?

—Each had their own room, says The Cousin, each their own bed.

Alice does not call. On the fourth floor it is said: *Georges has come.* —Where? —It happened in the dining room, I think, says my Cousin. Or elsewhere. I think there were some cookies and some mandarin liqueur on the round table. It was very intimate.

After, for the intimate tea with my Well-loved, there was port and some crème caramel. Or other secret cakes.

All the visitors on the fourth floor are not the dead. There are some who are neither living nor dead. That is the case of Father Christmas.

On the second floor Father Christmas does not exist. The very idea, no. What's marvellous about Father Christmas, the idea and the reality, is the very mystery of the impossible. For the impossible to be possible one merely has to go to the fourth floor. It makes one think: so there is in the impossible a possibility of the possible, how does one go from the unthinkable nothing-at-all to a perfectly sensible *Dasein*, of a fire-red colour, with great mobility, acting, leaving traces, more than probable. There is no such thing, he is not, and all of a sudden, like a star foretold, he passes, meteor or angel in the sky, crosses the whole fourth floor, leaving behind him a trail of dazzlings. I am not the only one to see him, to have seen him, to have believed I saw him, the others too, even if everyone differently, no one denies it, so many concrete elements a coat or a robe, red, a red that is a matter for discussion, I see him only from the back, others see him straight on, we have the experience of a profusion of testimony, even Eve my mother saw him, she makes him the model of one of the minuscule marionettes she creates for our little theatre. It's the easiest marionette to make, a single piece of red cloth, a hood in place of a face, whereas for the Hitler, another star of her theatre, one has to make the hair, the moustache, the eyes full of nastiness. The third floor doesn't express its opinion. As a stranger, according to the laws of hospitality, the door to the third floor must morally be opened for him, but Father Christmas is rich, he lacks rags, filth, smell, he gives, he's an anti-beggar. The higher one climbs —I say to myself —the more the concepts and the vigilance of the rationalities of the second and third floors, be it Jewish be it firmly secular, seem to dim and then dissipate. On the fourth floor one is in the *Midsummer's Night Dream and on Earth*, it is here that milk and honey flow without ration tickets, one has the right to desire, the world without war and hatred exists, no one everyone is is not JewishCatholicMuslim believing unbelieving there is no god, the childhood of Eve my mother is invited along with ours, the stairway is visited by Well-wishers, they are unknowns, elegantly dressed who give little girls gifts in which one will never be able to believe again, large dollhouses, miniature trains full of miniature travellers, and nobody overlooks the fact that on the Place d'Armes at the same moment, beneath the balconies of 54, march the troops of Marshall Pétain, but there is something pardoned on the fourth floor, and without our thinking about it, it is here that Universal Peace is saved for Future Times and not in the hidden shelters in the basement of rue Philippe where Eve and the children of the second floor descend when there is an air raid in the middle of the night. In truth on the fourth floor no one thinks anything. Everyone is content. For Dr Georges Cixous, republican secular Jew expelled stateless prohibited, dismissed by Nazism and Pétainism, the fourth floor if it could last would be the modest paradise of the people. Unfortunately the telephone requisitions, the Dr leaves.

It is truly Paradise. What is the true Paradise?

One only had to go to the fourth floor, when everyone was still alive. Cosmic government is a model of wisdom and compromise. The floors respect their political and philosophical differences. When the nonbelievers and the believers sit down together on the third floor, no one could say who believes what. Hostilities flare up only around the question of garlic. At the thought of this odour, the two grandmothers face off like two civilizations united by horror and war, a little death drive gets going, despised breath of Omi, expressions of disgust barely restrain themselves from using words that sting. On the third floor no one says 'the Ashkenazis', moreover no one knows this barbaric word, one thinks 'the Germans' and one doesn't say it. It is class struggle. But the parties of garlic and non-garlic are reconciled around homeopathy. Except for Eve my mother. And on the subject of Father Christmas

This Supernatural has an unlimited and welcoming resident's permit on the premises of the fourth floor. Since he lands on the terrace, the second floor does not even have to profess its secularism about his passage. He is not antisemitic. He is not Jewish. Nationality of Father Christmas: none. He is ideal. He foretells humanity to come. One keeps only love. One tries. 'He's coming!' I don't know in which language Mr Emile greets Him. 'Him' is the right name. Him, barely has he come than he is passed, a red-and-white flash quicker than lightning. Him comes from the right, that I can say: I turn my head, after all one doesn't see God, one 'sees' the passage, one doesn't see that one has seen before having seen. And not a second. No time for a thought. One doesn't think. One will think later. Several examples in the Bible of neither seeing nor thinking, instead of this human time the lightning strike of a bush. But in the Bible the Father lightning speaks, a strange voice both cosmic and internal, everywhere and nowhere. Our 'Him', not a word merely a frrmdeilmm, a rustle of cloth against the door, that I heard. No one would ever think of inviting him to lunch. Him is a visual manifestation of our desires, a heart throb. Oh! We are in love! It's over. I have had my illumination.

Let us move on to the remainders: the gifts. The word gift is a gift for the greedy imagination. My father gives it to me: a gift is a letter, a large elegant initial letter, a great figure of writing. I adore gifts. Him left fairy-like Letters for those who were crazy about riddles, children, poets, inventors, the seekers of secrets. First it's hidden, it's promising, behind the tree it promises, and then

then

I hear Mr Emile weeping. He weeps loudly, broadly, with angry sobs, he complains, Mr Job, if only he could beat up Father Christmas, drag him by his hood before the court, he rails against the Unjust, he shakes his insulted socks, he brandishes Carrots and Turnips, these projectiles, this excrement, these poison gifts, these obscene testimonies of the meanness of the Authorities, this repulsive sadism, carrots in his socks! The tears of Mr Emile extinguish the light of my joy,

The Cousin says: You saw him? Father Christmas? I say: A little. I don't dare say: I didn't see him, didn't look. The Cousin laughs: It was your father.

My father? The author of the fratricide? The killer with carrot and turnip?

Is that it, the pathetic violence of human nature?

In the jaws of the nightmare, the world suffocates, and it is not a dream! I understand nothing. To understand nothing is an intolerable suffering. Mr Emile laments like a donkey. Such pain suddenly hollows out a distance between us, Mr Emile is on the other side, I don't know where my father is, reality for whatt (*sic*)

Time stops, waits

—First you weep, then you laugh, says the Book.

I think that two months' worth two years have passed since the last line. I check. In fact, two weeks' worth two months have passed. I am coagulated. I don't understand myself. Separated from me? I slaved away at great pains on the last chapter of *Mdeilmm*. Certain mornings Mdeilmm enters onto the paper under the name Mleidmm, and I lose its trace. *Mdeilmm* is not finished, doesn't end. A few last pages, two or three, are recalcitrant, refuse absolutely to come out of their mute night. Too late. It's finished. Everything spectres. I'm waiting. In vain. Void-Void. Void.

No dream comes to help. I am void. Void. Widow of dreams. Instead of help, the storehouse sends me Incongruous Dreams. I don't want them, I say. Is that your way of mocking me, Spirit? Who is meddling with me? Who keeps me tied up for years' worth of night?

—Who are you, Void? —Some Latin

I wonder if it is not the enormous spirit of Alice, her face closed to me, her book bristling: she doesn't appreciate those who are not believers. She detests Eve!

—It's not because she is German that she is so stubborn. She must be watched. Says Alice, in the guise of Georges. What is more than regrettable is that my wife cannot join me in case of death. It is said that some of those among us have undergone a similar distress. One's merits count for nothing. For there is karma, dictates Georges, writes Alice. And he-she adds: What would we do without Alice?

And there I see her! There, in back to the right, lying on the whole table like a mocking jellyfish barely veiled, eyes half-closed. It's her Spirit, I should have thought of that. She says nothing to repulse me.

Might I one day —no—, might it happen one day that without any conversion or conviction, I begin to —I catch myself in a state of belief?

There have to be dead people, and their consent. Eve will never go along. That is why I adore her.

—And the beloved? says my daughter.

—Perhaps he comes, I say, and even often, but otherwise.

His way of coming back, unconventional. 'We will find another telephone,' he says.

—I am not going to let your hesitations overtake me, says the Book. I will go no farther.